# OLLIE SPARK

## AND THE
## ACCIDENTAL ADVENTURE

# OLLIE SPARK

## AND THE
## ACCIDENTAL ADVENTURE

GILLIAN CROSS
AND ALAN SNOW

David Fickling Books

31 Beaumont Street
Oxford OX1 2NP, UK

Ollie Spark and the Accidental Adventure
is a
DAVID FICKLING BOOK

First published in Great Britain in 2022 by
David Fickling Books,
31 Beaumont Street,
Oxford, OX1 2NP

www.davidficklingbooks.com

Text © Gillian Cross, 2022
Illustrations © Alan Snow, 2022

978-1-78845-239-7

1 3 5 7 9 10 8 6 4 2

DAVID FICKLING BOOKS Reg. No. 8340307

A CIP catalogue record for this book is available from the British Library.

Printed and bound in Great Britain by Clays, Ltd, Elcograf S.p.A.

*To Lyra*

*G.C.*

*To Errol*

*A.S.*

## Chapter 1
## The Van

I was up on the roof when Mum started shouting.

'Ollie! Come and mend the washing machine!'

She made me jump and I nearly dropped my mini-drone.

'I'll be there in a minute!' I shouted back. 'I'm just finishing the jackdaw scarer!'

I *had* to stop jackdaws falling down my bedroom chimney. It's already a squash in there, with me and three of my little cousins. There's no space for birds flapping around in a panic. They spray soot every-where, and the cousins all start screaming.

'But I need the machine *now*!' Mum yelled. 'The kitchen's full of dirty washing!'

'It's all right!' I shouted. 'I can fix it!' There are loads of people in our house, but I'm the only one who understands machines. I *love* them.

But I needed to finish the jackdaw scarer first.

It would only take a couple of minutes. The next time a jackdaw set foot on the chimney, it would start up the mini-drone and send me a signal. The drone would fly straight at the jackdaw and then chase it away – steered by my phone.

I'd spent days making the drone, and all I had to do now was fix a pressure pad on the chimney. Only had three more screws to go . . .

'The washing can't wait!' Mum shouted.

'Just coming!' I called. But as I reached for the first screw –

SCREECH!!!!

I nearly fell off the roof.

A huge green van swerved up our road. The driver was crunching the gears and shouting my name.

'Ollie! OLLIE!!! Look what I've got!'

It lurched to a stop outside our house and Aunt Caz jumped out. She waved her arms at the van, yelling, 'Look what I've got! Isn't it wonderful?'

It didn't look wonderful to me. I could hear at least three things wrong with the engine and one of the huge tyres was going flat. Even the name on the side was flaking off.

The other grown-ups came pouring out of the house, all trying to fit through the front door at once: Mum and Dad, Granny, Aunt Laura and Aunt Dionne, Grandad Peel and all the uncles. And two of my little cousins leaned out of the bedroom window, squealing with excitement. Everyone was talking at once.

'Where did you find it?'

'Can we go for a ride?'

'Caz, you're amazing!'

When people in my family get excited, they get *really* excited.

Aunt Caz stood by the van, looking modest. 'It'll be wonderful when it's finished. But it needs a bit of work.'

Suddenly, everyone was shouting my name. 'Ollie!' 'OLLIE!!' **'OLLIE!!!'** (Why do the words 'work' and 'Ollie' always go together?)

I sighed. Dropping the last three screws into my pocket, I tucked the mini-drone into my toolbelt and abseiled down from the roof. Before I even hit the ground, the grown-ups were crowding around, grinning and shouting at me.

'Look what Aunt Caz has found!'

'Isn't it huge?'

'It's going to be fantastic!'

I looked up at them all. Then I looked at the van. 'What is it *for*?' I said. 'And how did you pay for it?'

No one in our family ever has any money. They all stopped shouting and turned to look at Aunt Caz. She gave a huge, triumphant smile.

'Beddington Potts!' she said.

Chapter 2
With
Recipes!

All the grown-ups looked at each other. Then they looked back at Aunt Caz.

'What's Beddington Potts?' said Grandad Peel.

'He's my spy,' Aunt Caz said proudly. 'Faster than a rocket! Sharper than a needle!'

I didn't understand. 'What do you mean *your* spy?'

Aunt Caz's smile got bigger. 'I've found a publisher who wants me to write SIX Beddington Potts books. They've paid me some money already.'

Mum gave her a hug and everyone cheered – especially me. I love spy stories! And Aunt Caz was actually going to be *paid* for writing them. I couldn't wait to read about Beddington Potts!

'I hope you've bought us some cake,' Dad said. 'To celebrate.'

Aunt Caz laughed. 'There was no money left for cake. I spent it all on the van.'

Everyone stared.

'*All* of it?' Aunt Dionne said.

Aunt Caz nodded. She was still grinning.

'But –' I still didn't get it. 'Why did you buy the van?'

Aunt Caz put an arm round my shoulders. 'To live in, silly! So I can travel abroad to do research – and collect recipes.'

'Recipes?' said Uncle Rashid.

Aunt Caz gave another huge smile. 'That's my brilliant idea. They're going to be spy stories WITH RECIPES.'

'Yay!' shouted my cousins. They love food.

I looked at the van. 'You're going to live in *that*?'

'It needs a bit of work,' Aunt Caz said airily. 'But there's loads of space inside. I thought you could just do a few alterations . . . Look!' She pulled me towards the side of the van and tugged the doors open.

She was right about the space. But it wasn't the sort of space you could *live* in. There was nothing inside except rows and rows of empty bookshelves – and a battered old quad bike. (What was *that* for?)

Aunt Caz jumped into the van and stroked the front of the bike. 'They threw this in for nothing when I bought the van. Wasn't that nice?'

'Bet it doesn't work,' I said.

Aunt Caz beamed at me. 'I'm sure you can fix it! When you've done the alterations.' She patted my arm. 'Why don't you draw up some plans – while I go and start writing!'

She tossed me the keys and jumped out of the van. With a wave at my cousins, she swept into the house, leaving all the other grown-ups to follow.

I looked round the van. *Be sensible*, I told myself. *You haven't got time for anything extra.* There were hundreds of things in the house that needed fixing. And most of the week I had to be at school. I couldn't work on the van as well.

But . . .

I couldn't resist taking a look inside. And the moment I did, my brain started racing. *I could fix a flap-down table over there. With storage under the seats. If I take down the shelves, I'll have lots of wood. And that's a good place to fit in a toilet . . .*

I took out my notebook and pencil and unrolled my steel tape measure. No harm in making a few measurements and drawing some diagrams . . .

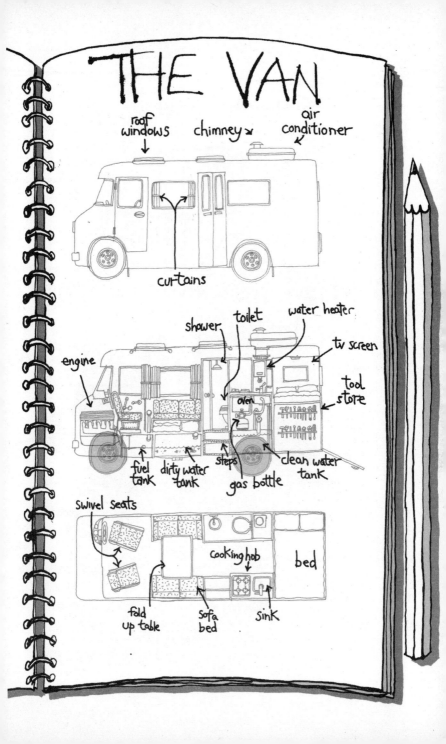

Chapter 3
The Stupid
Quad Bike!

Once I'd started, I couldn't stop thinking about the van. I fixed the engine first – to get that out of the way – and then started on the inside. Aunt Caz had spent all her money on the van (and that stupid broken-down quad bike!) so I had to hunt around in skips and junk yards to find what I needed.

Everyone else tried to help. Dad and Uncle Rashid went busking to earn money for a new tyre. Aunt Dionne made cushions and blinds (out of the dining room curtains) and Mum found spare mugs and dishes to go in the cupboards.

My cousins drew pictures of Beddington Potts to stick up on the walls. They gave him lots of different disguises. Huge dark glasses. Big false beards. A long black cloak and a hat that covered his eyes.

Aunt Caz loved the pictures – but they made her laugh. 'He couldn't sneak around in those things. Everyone would stare!'

*So what* would *he wear?* I wondered. *Would he dress like a postman? Or ride a delivery bike? Or . . .*

I thought about it while I worked on the van. That gave me lots of time to invent disguises for Beddington Potts. Aunt Caz had talked about 'a few alterations' – but I ended up redoing the whole of the inside. Most nights I was working till midnight. And sometimes I got up early, to do a bit more before school.

For the first three weeks, it felt as if the work would go on for ever. But suddenly, at the end of the fourth week – it was finished! I put down my screwdriver and looked round. Everything was perfect.

Except for the quad bike.

I'd kept asking Aunt Caz to move it, but it was still in the middle of the floor. In between the fold-up table and the shower. I stuck my head out of the door and yelled.

'I'll put the quad bike in the back garden!'

Aunt Caz came staggering out of the house, with her arms full of saucepans. 'Don't be silly,' she said. 'I'm taking it with me.' She dumped the saucepans on the table and patted my arm. 'I'm sure you'll find somewhere to put it. But be quick! I'm leaving this afternoon!' She ran back into the house and slammed the door.

I sighed and put the saucepans away in the cupboard. Then I took out my tape measure. The van had a big boot. Would the quad bike go in there? Maybe if I fitted a couple of brackets . . .

Half an hour later, I was right inside the boot, lashing the quad bike to the brackets. I tied the last knot and shook the bike to make sure it wouldn't rattle about. Then I sat back and grinned. Done. This time, I'd *really* finished!

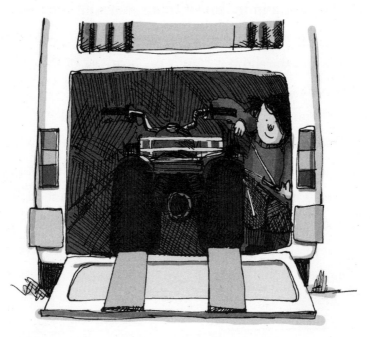

I had a stack of homework waiting upstairs, but I couldn't face doing anything else straight away. I was exhausted. Leaning my head against the side of the boot, I closed my eyes. Just for a moment . . .

I was woken by a loud SLAM! Everything was dark and I didn't know where I was – until I heard a rumble and the sound of gears grinding. Everything around me began to rattle and shake.

I was shut in the boot of the van – and Aunt Caz was driving away!

I kicked the tailgate, making as much noise as I could. But it was no use. The van rattled and thumped all the time. Aunt Caz was never going to notice the extra noise. I'd just have to wait till she stopped.

I knew Mum would worry if I wasn't there for tea, so I pulled out my phone and sent her a quick message.

> I'm with Aunt Caz. Don't worry.
> Everything is fine. xxx

She messaged me straight back.

> But the kettle has just broken!

> Try changing the fuse.
> Love you Mum xxx

I pressed send. Then I switched on my phone

torch and turned to the quad bike. No point in wasting time.

If I was stuck there, I might as well strip down the engine. *Thank goodness I got some new gaskets!* I thought.

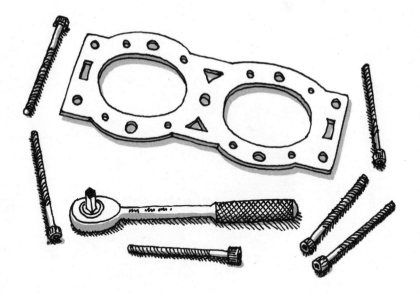

# The Quad Bike

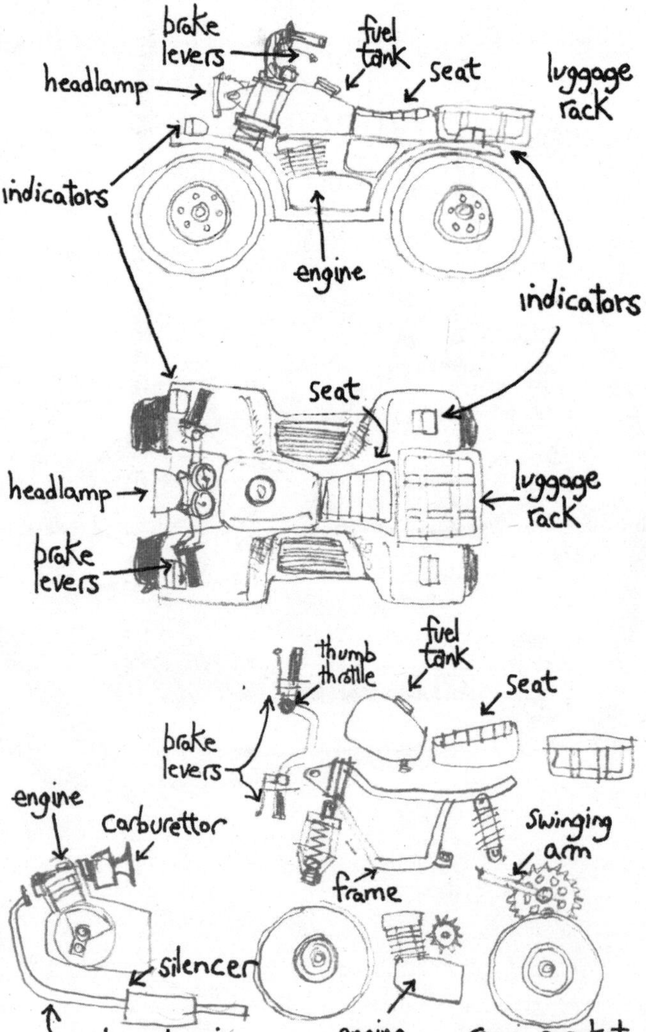

brake levers
fuel tank
headlamp
seat
luggage rack
indicators
engine
indicators

seat
headlamp
brake levers
luggage rack

thumb throttle
fuel tank
seat
brake levers
engine
carburettor
swinging arm
frame
silencer
exhaust pipe
engine
rear sprocket

# Chapter 4
# Where Are We?

It took *hours*. I had to unblock the fuel pipe and clean out the carburettor and change the spark plugs and fit a new head gasket. By the time I'd put everything back together, I was exhausted. I settled down to read all the messages that had pinged in while I was working.

But where IS the fuse?
Mum xxx

Ollie, I've broken the needle on my
sewing machine!!! Aunt Dionne x

My computer's frozen in the middle
of Level 17

My bike's got a flat tyre and the
chain's snapped!

The boiler's stopped working – and
the house is FREEZING!!! What do I
need to do? Dad xxx

There were loads more like that. I was just going
to start answering them – when the van stuttered to
a stop. I kicked the tailgate again, as hard as I could.

This time, Aunt Caz heard me. She jumped out
and came running to open the boot. 'Ollie!' she

gasped. 'What are you doing in there?'

'I was fixing some brackets,' I said. 'And you shut me in and–'

'Well, thank goodness you're here!' Aunt Caz said frantically. 'The engine's stopped and I don't know why. Can you come and see?'

My family think I can mend anything. But there are some problems you can't fix with a screwdriver.

I could see what was wrong the moment I switched on the engine.

'We've run out of fuel,' I said.

Aunt Caz looked annoyed.

'But I filled up! As soon as I drove off the ferry.'

'The *ferry*?' I stared at her. 'Where are we?'

'Somewhere abroad,' Aunt Caz flapped her hand impatiently. 'How should I know? I've been driving all night.'

I took out my phone to check our location. There were even more messages, but I hadn't got time to read them. What I needed was a signal. And there was nothing. Not even one bar.

I climbed out of the van and looked around. We were on top of a high hill, with a strange, dead forest on both sides. Ahead of us, the road zigzagged down – almost vertically – to a valley full of thick, dark fog.

I couldn't see through to the bottom of the valley. The fog was too thick. But rising out of it were hundreds of tall, spindly towers, gleaming in the early morning sun.

Aunt Caz clutched my arm. 'It's a city! We must be able to get petrol there.'

I looked down at the towers. 'It's a long way to walk,' I said.

'Who's walking?' Aunt Caz grinned. 'We don't need petrol to go *down*. I just have to take off the brake!'

'But you can't –'

Too late! Aunt Caz was already climbing into the van. I didn't want to be left behind! Scrambling into the passenger seat, I started fastening my seat belt. Before it clicked, Aunt Caz took off the handbrake and we started moving,

V·E·R·Y–S·L·O·W·L·Y–A·T–F·I·R·S·T
AND THEN FASTER AND FASTER
ANDFASTERANDFASTERANDFASTER......

I held on to the dashboard as we skidded round the zigzags. I was sure we were going to come off the road – but Aunt Caz was loving it.

'YAY!' she shouted. 'Isn't this great? I'll put it in in my book! Beddington Potts is a fantastic driver – faster than a rocket!'

'Not in a van like this!' I yelled.

Aunt Caz shrieked with laughter. 'OK. So design him a supercar!'

*Yeah, I'd love that – but not right now!* Just then, I was too busy worrying about the brakes on the van.

Suppose they failed? What would happen when we got to the bottom of the hill?

## Chapter 5
## Smog City

As the road levelled out, I heard Aunt Caz gasp and pump the brake pedal.

'It's not doing anything!' she wailed.

By then, we were into the fog. It was so thick we couldn't see more than a couple of metres ahead.

'Steer!' I shouted. 'Keep steering till the van stops by itself!'

We plunged into a tangle of narrow streets, with buildings on either side. Terraced houses . . . petrol station . . . school . . . Aunt Caz steered frantically left – right – right – left – left, round bends and over crossroads. There was lots of furious hooting, but we couldn't see any of the other vehicles, because of the fog.

Right – left – left – right – right . . . shops . . . flats . . . petrol station . . .

Gradually the van slowed down. At last it stopped, in the middle of a little square. I couldn't see much through the fog, but there was a café on one side, with some kind of park next to it. Aunt Caz gave a huge sigh of relief and flopped forward over the steering wheel.

'We need to get some fuel,' I said. I opened the van door, and –

POW! Thick fog swirled into the van. It went into my mouth and up my nose, almost suffocating me. I slammed the door shut again, but it was too late. The van was full of the horrible, choking stink.

'EUGH!' Aunt Caz sat up, pulling a face. 'We can't stay here. Let's get inside that café – fast!'

She slid out of the van and raced into the café – leaving the keys behind. I had a quick look round, to make sure she hadn't forgotten anything else. Then I locked the van, put the keys in my pocket and followed her inside.

By the time I got there, she was already sitting at a table, with a waiter pointing out things on the menu. As I sat down, the waiter nodded and went off to the kitchen.

Aunt Caz beamed at me. 'Ready for breakfast?'

I nodded. 'I'm really hungry. What did you order?'

'How should I know? I couldn't understand the menu, so I just pointed at lots of things.' Aunt Caz looked round happily. 'Beddington Potts would *love* this place.'

I stared out at the fog. 'Really?'

Aunt Caz nodded. 'You can't see a *thing* out there! It could be full of enemy agents, meeting in dark corners. Making evil plans!' There was a huge grin on her face. 'Beddington Potts has eyes like a hawk. He'd be slipping through the smog, finding clues everywhere.'

'When he can't *see* anything?' I said.

'I'm going to give him lots of special gadgets, like . . . a secret camera and . . . and a hidden microphone . . . and . . . and . . .' Aunt Caz waved her hands around, struggling to think of some more.

'How about a mini-drone?' I said. 'Like the one I made for my jackdaw scarer.' I pulled it out of my toolbelt to show her.

Her eyes gleamed. 'That's perfect! I can just imagine it, flying through the smog. Spotting hidden clues!'

Opening her little backpack, she pulled out a blue

notebook labelled *Recipes and Useful Words*. She wrote her title on the first clean page, in big, black letters:

**THE EVIL SMOG**

Then she started scribbling a list of words: *foggy hazy claggy smog blurred grey peasouper mysterious choking stink* . . . She'd covered half a page by the time the waiter brought our food.

He had a big tray full of dishes and he said their names as he put them down on the table. I didn't understand any of the names – but I could smell what was in the food.

Turnips.

There was turnip stew, mashed turnips, roast turnips, turnip chips, pickled turnips – at least eight different things – but they were *all* made of turnips. *Aunt Caz will be disappointed*, I thought.

But she grinned and started spooning things on to her plate. 'Come on, Ollie!' she said. 'Tuck in!'

I shoved the drone into my pocket and took some turnip chips. But before I'd even tasted them Aunt Caz gave a gasp of excitement.

'This turnip pickle is AMAZING!' she said. 'I must get the recipe for my book!'

She jumped up, grabbed her notebook and raced through the swing door into the kitchen.

I couldn't see any point in following her, so I took a spoonful of pickled turnips and started chewing. They weren't *totally* awful. Maybe I could get used to the taste of turnips. *I'll keep trying till Aunt Caz comes back*, I thought.

But she didn't come back.

## Chapter 6
## Disappeared!

After half an hour, the waiter brought a bill. I tried to tell him Aunt Caz was in the kitchen, but when I stood up – to go and fetch her – he slapped the bill down on the table and held out his hand.

I couldn't understand a word he was saying, but I could see he was cross. He wasn't going to let me move until that bill was paid.

Where *was* Aunt Caz?

I needed to go and find her. But when I turned

towards the kitchen door, the waiter shook his head, blocking my way.

I sat down again, feeling frustrated. *Why did I let him stop me?* I thought, *I should have moved faster – like Beddington Potts.* He would have been in the kitchen already, tracking down Aunt Caz. That was what I needed to do. I had to *investigate*.

There was only one way to do that. I had to trick the waiter . . .

I thought it out carefully. Then I found the credit card in Aunt Caz's backpack, paid the bill, and picked up the backpack, as if I was going to leave. But the moment the waiter moved off –

I sneaked the other way! I crept through the kitchen door, before anyone could stop me.

The kitchen was full of steam. There were three chefs stirring saucepans, two chopping turnips, and two more carrying a dustbin through the back door. But there was nobody else in there.

'Where's my aunt?' I said.

The chefs all looked at each other, shaking

their heads. Had they understood? I couldn't tell, so I looked in Aunt Caz's backpack and found her passport.

'Look! My aunt!' I said. 'Where did she go?'

I pointed at the passport and waved my arms around, to show what I meant. The biggest chef came over and peered at Aunt Caz's picture.

'Ah!' he said slowly. '*Ah!*' He thought for a moment and then he said something I couldn't understand – and pointed at the back door.

She'd gone? Without me? That didn't sound like Aunt Caz. I went across to the back door and took a look outside. There was no one in sight, except the two chefs with the dustbin. They were lifting it into a muddy old four-by-four with leaves tangled round the spare wheel.

'Hey!' I called. 'Have you seen my aunt?' I held up the passport to show them.

They looked at each other. Then they muttered something and pointed away from the four-by-four, up the road behind me.

I looked over my shoulder, peering into the fog. I couldn't see anyone at all. If only I could understand what they said! '*When* did she go?' I said.

They obviously didn't understand *me* either, so I went back into the kitchen – and suddenly spotted something.

There on the kitchen table was a battered old cookery book, with a big green leaf sticking out like a bookmark. And underneath that book, I could see the corner of another one. A small blue notebook . . .

I reached out to move the cookery book – but the big chef was quicker than I was. He snatched it up and held it to his chest, as if it was the most valuable thing in the world. That was weird – but I didn't care about the cookery book. It was the notebook I wanted. I grabbed it as fast as I could. And there were the words on the front, written in Aunt Caz's wild, spidery writing. *Recipes and Useful Words.*

It was Aunt Caz's notebook all right. She would never have left that behind. So the chefs were lying!

Where was she? Had they hidden her somewhere in the kitchen? I snatched up the notebook and looked round frantically. She couldn't be in a cupboard, because they all had glass doors. Maybe that

big fridge –

I raced across and tugged the door open. A wave of cold air hit me in the face and I staggered backwards, but not before I'd seen what was inside.

Turnips. A big heap of turnips. With a bunch of strange green leaves lying on top of them.

I stared at the leaves for a moment, trying to think straight. Aunt Caz wasn't in there. So she couldn't be anywhere in the kitchen. And they hadn't taken her out through the restaurant, or I would have seen. So that only left the back door and –

The dustbin!

They must have put her in the dustbin! That was

why there were two chefs carrying it out! It must have been too heavy for one of them to lift on his own!

I raced through the back door again – but I was too late. The four-by-four had left the road. It was rattling away through the park beside the café. I ran after it, but it was going much too fast. After a couple of seconds, its tail-lights disappeared into the smog.

They'd kidnapped Aunt Caz!

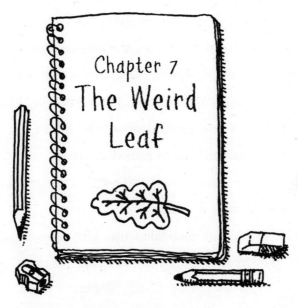

Chapter 7
The Weird Leaf

What was I going to do? I didn't want to worry Mum and Dad, but I thought I'd better call them, so I sat down on a tree stump and pulled out my phone.

The battery was dead.

I put my head in my hands. How bad could things get? I was in a foreign country. All on my own. Someone had kidnapped Aunt Caz and I had to rescue her – but how could I, when I didn't understand a word anyone said?

If only Beddington Potts was here! He'd probably have picked up the language by now.

I made myself take a long, deep breath. I wasn't Beddington Potts. But I could try to act like him. Faster than a rocket! Sharper than a needle! I had to hunt for clues that would lead me to Aunt Caz.

I stood up and looked round the park.

That was when I realized what a weird place it was. Everything was dead.

The grass had shrivelled up. The trees were just bare, jagged branches disappearing into the smog.

Wherever I looked, all the plants were withered and dry. I couldn't see anything green at all.

Except for one tiny spot in a little patch of mud.

What was that? I got up and went to see. There was a single green leaf, lying in the middle of the mud. In the tyre marks where the four-by-four had gone through. I bent down to pick it up and thought, *Weird!*

It was the same odd shape as the leaf in that cookery book. And the leaves in the fridge, lying on top of the turnips – they were that shape too. And I'd seen some more as well, but I couldn't remember where. Was that just a coincidence? Or was it –

A CLUE???

Suddenly, my brain went into hyperdrive, bursting with questions.

What did all these leaves mean?

And where did they come from?

They hadn't been growing in the park. All the plants in the park were dead.

AND – I stared at the leaf in my hand – *why wasn't this one squashed?*

That was the weirdest thing of all. I'd found that leaf lying in the tyre tracks of the four-by-four. But it wasn't squashed into the mud. *Why not?* There was only one possible answer. It must have fallen into the mud after the tyres had gone past. But that was impossible. There was nowhere for it to have come from. Unless –

YES!

The memory exploded, like a flash of lightning in my brain! *That* was the other place I'd seen those leaves. Lots of them. They were tangled round the four-by-four's spare wheel! The one in my hand must have fallen off as it drove through the mud. And if *one* leaf had fallen –

I looked up quickly and – YES! There was another leaf, just ahead. And another one after that, almost hidden in the fog. I'd found the clue I needed. I could follow the trail of leaves!

I almost started straight away, racing across the park as if I really was Beddington Potts. But – just in time – I realized that wouldn't work. I couldn't run fast enough to overtake the four-by-four. And the trail might go on for hundreds of kilometres. How far could I run before I collapsed with exhaustion?

I stared down at the leaf I was holding. If only I was old enough to drive the van!

But that wasn't the answer either. Even Beddington Potts couldn't go off-roading in a mobile library.

*But he could –*

Of course! What an idiot I was! I pushed the leaf into my top pocket and started running. Not following the leaf trail, but racing the other way, out of the park and back to the nearest petrol station.

If I had some petrol, I could follow the trail on the quad bike! Faster than a rocket!

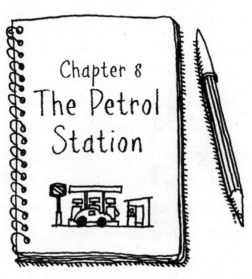

Chapter 8
The Petrol
Station

By the time I reached the petrol station, I was almost out of breath. I went into the shop, snatched a petrol can off the shelf and took out Aunt Caz's credit card. Then I went to the counter and waved the card, pointing at the pump to show I wanted to fill the can.

The man behind the counter pulled a face and started shaking his head. What was wrong? Was I too young to buy petrol?

It was looking that way – when the man's face

suddenly changed. He leaned forward, over the counter, stared at the front of my jacket for a moment and then came round and took the petrol can I was holding.

What on earth –?

I was too surprised to move. I just stood there as he went outside to the pump and filled the petrol can. Then he came back and handed it back to me, wagging his finger, as if he was telling me to be careful.

I couldn't say anything he would understand, so I just smiled and held up the credit card, to show I was ready to pay.

And something even stranger happened.

The man glanced at my jacket again. Then he waved the credit card away. It was absolutely clear what he meant. He didn't want any money from me. Not for the petrol. Not even for the can. He just winked and pointed at the door, to show I could go.

I didn't understand. But I remembered what Uncle Rashid always said: *Don't waste your luck!* And I hadn't got time to stand around wondering. I had

to get on the trail of that four-by-four. So I gave him a big smile, to say thank you, and turned round to leave the shop.

As I went, I caught sight of my reflection in the door. And I suddenly saw what the man had been staring at. It was the leaf I'd picked up in the park. I'd tucked it into my pocket, but the top was sticking out and the shape was quite clear. He'd given me the petrol – for nothing – *because I was showing the leaf.*

I knew I'd found another clue – but why were the leaves so important? *I need to be sharper!* I thought as I lugged the heavy petrol can back down the road. *I need to think like a spy!*

When I got back to the van, I unlocked the boot and heaved the bike off its brackets. Then I eased it down on to the road, filled the fuel tank and locked

the empty petrol can into the boot.

*Right,* I thought. *Here we go! Faster than a rocket!*

I wheeled the bike into the park, strapped up my helmet and climbed on. When I turned the key, the engine started straight away, running sweet and true. Then I opened the throttle and I was off, plunging into the fog.

Following the leaf trail to track down the four-by-four – and rescue Aunt Caz!

## Chapter 9
## Trapped

It was hard to breathe. The foggy air was thick and still, smelling of soot and decay and dust. And there was a strange noise ahead of me – a continuous low rumble – but I couldn't stop to work out what it was. I had to keep looking out for the next leaf.

And the next . . . and the next . . . By the time I'd been going for twenty minutes, I was really good at spotting them.

But then they stopped. Suddenly there was no

green dot ahead of me. Nothing to the left, either. And nothing to the right.

Should I carry on in the same direction? Or hunt for wheel tracks? I stopped the quad bike and got off to look round. The four-by-four *must* have come that way, but there was no sign of it.

What was I going to do? If only Dad was here. Or Mum. Or even one of my little cousins. At home, there was always someone around if you needed to talk. But here there was nobody. I was all alone, with no idea what to do next.

I was standing next to a little playground, with a slide and swings and a roundabout. Very ordinary – except there weren't any children playing there. And I could see why. Everything was covered with soot and dust. The slide was rusting away and the swings were broken and dirty.

*Someone needs to fix those*, I thought. But not me. I had to rescue Aunt Caz.

I was just turning away from the playground when there was a noise. I could only just hear it over the rumbling ahead, but it sounded like a groan. Or a low, exhausted whine.

*I haven't got time –*

But some noises you can't walk away from. I opened the filthy little gate and went into the playground. The noise seemed to be coming from the roundabout.

From *inside* the roundabout.

**???**

I went across to look. It took me a minute or two to work out what had happened. A couple of the planks on top of the roundabout were loose at one end. If you stepped on them, they'd bend down, and if you weren't very big – *WHOOSH*! You'd fall into the roundabout.

Then – what?

You'd try to push your way out, of course. But if you pushed from underneath, the planks wouldn't go *up*. They'd hit the metal bar on top – and you'd be trapped. You could only get out by pulling the planks *down*.

But a little child would never work that out.

I kneeled down and shouted into the roundabout. 'It's no good pushing. You need to *pull*!'

The only answer was another tired whine.

'PULL!' I yelled.

Nothing. Not even a sound this time.

I had to do something. I didn't dare to push at the boards from above. That could hurt whoever was trapped inside. So I took a screwdriver out of my

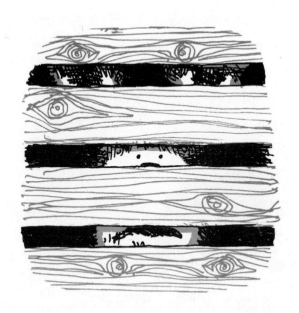

toolbelt and started undoing the metal bar. I slid it
sideways, just enough to get my fingers round the end
of the planks – and pulled them *UP*!

They bent backwards and snapped off in my
hands, leaving a hole in the top of the roundabout.

For a second there was silence. Then a head came
up through the hole.

And it wasn't a child at all.

It was a dog.

## Chapter 10
## Grabbed

It was a *very tired* dog, with only just enough strength left to lick my hand. Certainly not enough to climb out of the roundabout. I could see I needed to help.

Very carefully, I bent down and reached into the hole. My arms scraped against the sides, but I managed to lift the dog out on to the ground.

He could hardly stand.

'You're safe now,' I said. 'Go home.' I patted his head, very gently, and stepped back.

He didn't move. Just stared up at me with big, tired eyes.

'Go on,' I said. 'Someone must be worrying about you.'

I hoped that was true. But he just kept staring.

What could I do? I wanted to stay and look after him, but I *had* to find Aunt Caz. I made myself turn away and walk out of the playground.

When I reached the quad bike, I looked round – and there was the dog, plodding after me. Limping slightly, as if he'd hurt one of his paws. He looked exhausted. If he'd been in the roundabout for long, he must be very hungry. And thirsty too. But he kept on walking towards me.

Why didn't he go home?

*Maybe he hasn't got anyone,* I thought suddenly. *Maybe he's all on his own. Like me.*

I stood still, watching him come. When he reached the bike, I climbed on and patted the seat beside me. 'OK,' I said. 'You win.'

The dog grinned and wagged his tail, but he was too tired to jump up. I had to get down and lift him on to the seat. He settled down next to me, putting his head in my lap and I started the bike, peering into the fog as we began to move.

I was hoping to see another leaf. Just one more. To let me know I was going in the right direction. But I couldn't see a single speck of green.

Instead, the rumbling noise got louder and louder. And then I saw a huge dark mass blocking the way ahead. It was a long building, with hardly any windows. At one end was a tower, disappearing up into the fog. And all round the building was a vast car park, crammed with cars and vans and lorries.

Was the four-by-four there? Had they taken Aunt Caz into that building? I didn't know, but I was going to find out!

I parked the bike on the edge of the car park, got down and took off my helmet. Then I hoisted Aunt Caz's backpack on to my shoulders. I thought the dog would stay where he was, but as soon as I started moving he jumped down and followed me.

'OK,' I said. 'Just be quiet. Right?'

I started creeping round the car park, with the dog padding after me. I couldn't see far, because of the fog, but I went up and down the rows, hunting for the battered old four-by-four. Or a leaf. Or anything that would tell me I was on the right track.

I was about halfway round when suddenly, without any warning, two figures leaped out at me, from behind a lorry. One of them grabbed me round the neck and the other one shouted into my face. But I couldn't understand a word he was saying.

'Let me go!' I yelled. 'I'm not doing anything wrong!' How could I make them understand?

The dog started growling, and the man who was shouting kicked out at him. Then he nodded to the other one and the two of them started dragging me towards the edge of the car park. Were they going to let me go? I felt the arm round my neck start to loosen and I got ready to run.

But before I could get away, something weird happened.

One of the men suddenly stopped and pointed at my jacket. He was looking at the leaf in the pocket. Why? What was so special about it?

Whatever it was, it changed everything. The two

men muttered together for a moment. Then they started dragging me back through the car park. I struggled as hard as I could, and the dog snapped at their boots, but it was no use. They just kicked out at the dog and then picked me up and carried me through a door.

Into the huge dark building – and the rumbling, roaring noise.

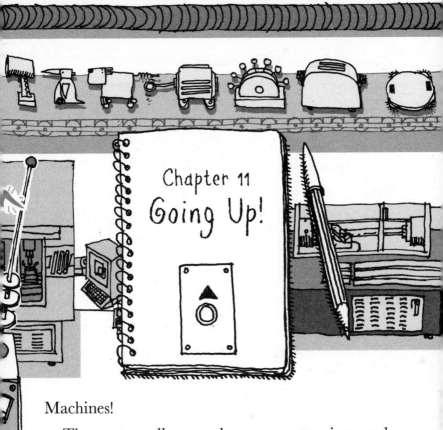

## Chapter 11
## Going Up!

Machines!

They were all around us, cogs turning, rods pounding up and down, conveyor belts churning past, carrying thousands of objects. It was deafening and amazing – and perfectly engineered. Normally, I'd have stood and stared at it all.

But nothing was normal. I was being hauled through the factory, so fast I could hardly stay on my feet, and I had no idea what was going on. Why had

the men grabbed me? Where were we going?

I was scared.

They marched me down the factory floor and pushed me into a lift. As the lift doors closed, one of them gave an angry shout. I didn't understand what he said, but I felt something warm rub against my leg and a wet tongue licked my hand. *Stupid dog,* I thought. *You could have run away.*

But I was glad he hadn't. It meant I wasn't alone. I couldn't pat him, because the men were gripping my arms, but I looked down and smiled. He licked my hand again and then peered round the lift, as if he was trying to work out why we were there.

*Wish I knew*, I thought. It must have something to do with the weird green leaf. Why had seeing the leaf made the men so angry? If only I could understand what they said! They were frowning and muttering to each other as if they were nervous about what was going to happen.

The lift was travelling fast, but it was still almost a minute before it started braking. I remembered the tower I'd seen, disappearing up into the mist. *We must be right at the top*, I thought, as the lift stopped.

The doors opened and the men dragged me out into a wide lobby, totally different from the factory. It was spacious and *quiet*, with paintings on the walls and a chandelier hanging from the ceiling. On the far side of the lobby was a big, panelled door.

Still whispering to each other, the men dragged me towards the door. They sounded *very* nervous now and they kept kicking out at the dog to stop him following us. But he wasn't put off. He stayed just out of range of their boots, trotting along behind us.

One of the men rang a bell beside the door. It

swung open and they pushed me forward.

'Come on, dog!' I shouted over my shoulder. Then I turned to walk through the door – and my mouth dropped open.

The room beyond was full of light. Bright sunshine streamed in through the windows and outside I could see blue sky, with no clouds – and no sign of smog.

I was so busy staring, that I didn't notice the man behind the desk. He let me look for a moment and then he stood up. He was short and round, with a shiny bald head, and he looked at me over the top of his glasses.

'Why are you wearing the Leaf?' he said.

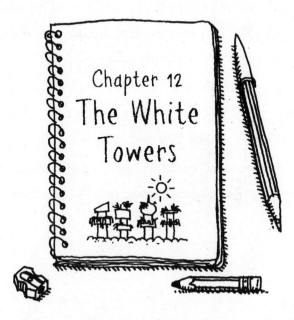

## Chapter 12
## The White Towers

'I – what?' *I actually understood what he was saying.* For a second, I was so relieved I couldn't speak.

The man smiled. 'I speak twelve languages and understand three more. Did you think I was an ignorant Groundling?'

I had no idea what he meant. 'What's a Groundling?'

He beckoned me across to the biggest window and pointed down. Suddenly I understood why I hadn't seen any smog through the window. The lift had taken us *above* it. We were high up, in the clear blue sky, at the top of a very tall tower.

There were dozens of other towers in the sky around us. They were all white – and beautiful. Round towers, with pointed turrets and tall arched windows. Square, modern towers, with whole walls made of glass. Fancy, decorated towers, like fairy palaces.

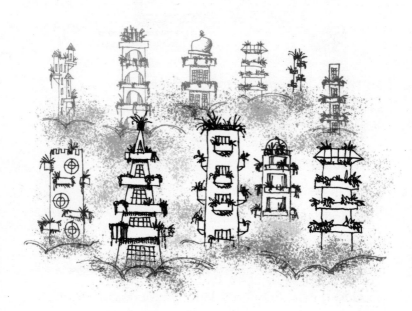

Every tower was different, but they all had gardens. I could see balconies crammed with plants. Tomatoes growing on flat roofs. Big bunches of grapes. Long green beans and bright red peppers.

That was strange enough, but there was something even odder. In among all the plants, most of the balconies had – *treadmills*. What were those doing there?

The man saw me staring, and he grinned. 'Everyone needs exercise. And it's a long way down to the ground. So people usually do their running up here.'

'You mean people *live* up here?'

'Some of us do,' the man said. 'I live over there.' He pointed at the nearest tower – and suddenly started waving.

For a moment I couldn't think what he was doing. Then I saw a little girl on the balcony. She was smiling and jumping up and down as she waved back at him.

'Is that your daughter?' I said.

'One of them.' The man smiled and blew her a kiss. 'The others are at school. In that tower.' He pointed the other way, towards a bigger tower, with lots of different balconies.

'So are you the Groundlings?' I said. 'The people who live up here?'

The man laughed. 'No, the Groundlings choose to live lower down.' He pointed into the smog. 'It's easier for them, because they work in my factory. And in the power station and the mine. I make sure they have everything they need down there – homes and shops and schools for their children. And the whole city runs smoothly. Like a beautiful machine.'

'I like machines,' I said.

The man smiled again. 'Me too.' His eyes flicked back to my pocket. 'So tell me – why are you wearing the Leaf?'

The dog whined suddenly. I didn't know why, but I patted his head, to let him know things were OK.

'I – I'm not *wearing* the leaf,' I said. 'I've got it in my pocket because it's a clue.'

'A *clue*?' The man raised his eyebrows. 'What kind of clue?'

'It's complicated.' How much should I tell him?

'No need to rush,' the man said. Pressing a button on his desk, he rattled off a string of words into the intercom. Then he waved at some sofas on the other side of the room. 'Please. Sit down, Mr –?'

'Ollie,' I said. 'My name's Ollie.' I sat down on one of the big, squashy sofas.

The man nodded. 'And your dog?'

'He's not –' *He's not mine*, I was going to say. But the dog came and laid his nose on my knee. To let me know I was wrong. He was mine now –

and he needed a name.

I said the first word that came into my head. 'He's called Gasket.'

'Gasket.' The man reached out and patted him. 'Good afternoon, Ollie and Gasket. I am Erebus Nyx. Owner of this factory – and the mine and power station that keep it running. And I think I may be able to help you.'

He sat down on the other sofa, facing me. The door opened and in came a woman carrying a tray loaded with glasses of juice, and plates full of cakes and cookies and fruit.

'Thank you, Selina.' Mr Nyx waved a hand and the woman put the tray down on the coffee table between us.

It seemed a long time since breakfast. And the food on the tray looked much better than turnips. As the woman went out, Mr Nyx smiled and pointed at the tray.

'Help yourself,' he said, 'while I tell you about the People of the Leaf.'

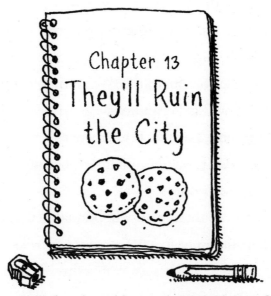

Chapter 13

They'll Ruin the City

I took a couple of cookies and gave one to Gasket, listening hard to what Mr Nyx was saying.

'This is a well-run, successful city,' he began. 'Everyone works hard. The city guards keep order. The factory and the power station and the mine all make a profit. It should be the perfect place to live. But we have a problem.' He shook his head sadly.

'The People of the Leaf?' I said.

Mr Nyx nodded. 'They are plotting to take over the city. And ruin it.'

I stared at him. 'You mean – they're *dangerous*?' My heart gave a huge, sickening thump. 'But . . . my aunt . . .'

Mr Nyx leaned forward. 'Why don't you tell me all about it? Maybe I can help.'

For a second, I couldn't think where to start. Then I started talking – faster and faster, because it was a relief to tell someone.

'There were these men who kidnapped my Aunt Caz when she went to ask for a turnip pickle recipe . . . and they carried her away in a dustbin and drove off in a four-by-four . . . and I'm trying to rescue her and I saw there were *lots* of leaves so I was following the trail of leaves to try and catch up . . . only the leaves stopped and I couldn't find any more and I was looking in your car park to see if the four-by-four was there and those men grabbed me and . . . and . . .'

I stuttered to a stop, staring at Mr Nyx.

Could he really help?

'That sounds like the People of the Leaf,' he said.

'But why would they kidnap Aunt Caz?' I didn't understand. 'She only wanted a pickle recipe!'

'Maybe she heard them discussing their plans,' Mr Nyx said. 'So they kidnapped her, to stop her telling anyone.'

I tried to stay calm, but I could feel my heart thumping. 'Do you think she's in danger?'

'I'm afraid so.' Mr Nyx leaned forward. 'You need to rescue her, Ollie.'

'*Me?* What can *I* do?'

'I think you can save your aunt – with my help.' Mr Nyx reached towards Gasket, as if he was going to pat him, but Gasket edged closer to me, nudging my knees with his head. *Silly dog,* I thought, stroking his ears.

I was starting to feel better. A couple of hours ago, I'd been all on my own, in the middle of the smog. Now I had Gasket with me, and Mr Nyx sounded ready to help me. 'Will you talk to the city guards?' I said. 'And get them to rescue Aunt Caz?'

Mr Nyx sighed and shook his head. 'That's too risky, Ollie. The People of the Leaf are merciless. If they see the guards, they'll think your aunt is putting them in danger. And they might . . .' His voice died away, as if the sentence was too terrible to finish.

That was seriously scary. Gasket licked my hand, and I tried to keep calm and *think*. What would Beddington Potts do? Would he put on a disguise and go after the kidnappers? There must be a way . . .

Mr Nyx was watching my face. 'What we need,' he said slowly, 'is someone who doesn't seem dangerous. Someone the People of the Leaf won't see as a threat, because . . .' he hesitated for a second, 'because he's just a boy on his own, trying to find his aunt!'

'You mean – you want me to go *by myself*?' I didn't get it. 'But – you said you'd help me!'

'I *will* help you,' Mr Nyx said. 'But you have to start by going on your own – if you're brave enough. I'll show you.'

He stood up and walked over to a big map on the

wall behind his desk.

'Here's the city.' he said, 'We're *here*, on the south side, in my factory. There's the power station, a bit further north, and then the mine, just outside the city boundary. And up *there*, in these mountains,' he pointed to the top of the map, 'is where the People of the Leaf hide out.'

'If you know where they are, can't you send the guards there?' I said.

'We've tried that.' Mr Nyx gave a little, unhappy laugh. 'We've tried dozens of times. But there's a huge network of caves under the mountains. And the People of the Leaf have lots of lookouts. If they see guards anywhere near their hideout, they move somewhere else. Underground. We don't stand a chance of catching them – unless we know *exactly* where they are.'

I frowned. 'If the guards can't find them, how can *I* possibly do it?'

'Because *they'll* find *you!*' Mr Nyx smiled suddenly. 'Their lookouts will see you – and they'll want to

know who you are. If you tell them you're looking for your aunt, I think they'll kidnap you too. So you don't cause any trouble.'

I didn't get it. 'And that's good? Me being kidnapped?'

'It's perfect!' Mr Nyx chuckled. 'Because you'll be wearing *this*.' He opened his desk drawer and took out a round blue badge with UNITED FOR EVER! blazoned across a football. 'Half the kids in the city wear badges like this. But this one is different. It's got a microchip on the back.'

'You mean . . . so you can track me?'

He nodded. 'We'll monitor where you are. And if you stop moving for more than two hours – I'll send in the guards. This time they'll know *exactly* where to go, and they'll come in so fast the People of the Leaf don't have a chance to escape.'

I thought about it. 'And Aunt Caz?'

'They'll rescue her. And you too, of course.' Mr Nyx turned round. 'Will you do it, Ollie? Will you be my secret agent?'

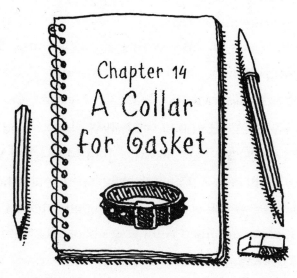

Chapter 14
A Collar
for Gasket

He was asking me to be a spy? Like Beddington
Potts? For a second, I felt terrified. *I can't do that.*

OK, I'd worked out how to follow the leaf trail.
But that wasn't *spying*. I'd just asked myself the right
questions and fitted the answers together – a bit like
fixing a machine.

Spying was different. It was fast and dangerous.
Spies lived in a world of treachery and car chases,
where anything could happen. *I can't...*

Mr Nyx was watching my face. 'What do you say? Will you do it, Ollie?'

*I can't . . .*

But it was my only chance to rescue Aunt Caz. I stood up straight and took a deep breath. 'Yes! I will!'

'You're a brave boy.' Mr Nyx came over and pinned the badge on to my pocket. 'Let's think what else you need. Take some of that food. And you'll need some water. It's a long way to the mountains.'

He spoke into the intercom again, and I picked up a plate and filled Aunt Caz's backpack with fruit and cookies. As I did up the straps, there was a tap on the door.

'Come!' called Mr Nyx.

Selina came in with a bottle of water and a small cardboard box. She tucked the water into the backpack and handed the box to Mr Nyx.

He looked down at Gasket. 'Your dog needs a collar.'

'A collar?' I didn't understand.

'City regulations,' Mr Nyx said. 'You don't want

to get stopped by the guards.'

He opened the box and took out a brown leather dog collar decorated with big metal studs. But when he bent down to strap it on, Gasket took a step back, stiff-legged, and growled.

'Gasket!' I shook my head at him. 'Don't be silly.'

He looked at me and then back at the collar.

'Maybe I'd better do it,' I said.

I took the collar out of Mr Nyx's hand – and nearly dropped it. It was heavier than I expected. I strapped it on and gave Gasket a pat.

Mr Nyx smiled and walked back to the map. 'Right. Now look at this. Here's the best way out of the city.' He traced the line with his finger. 'Cross the factory car park. Then follow this alley between the houses. From the end of that, you can see the chimneys of the power station. The mine is just beyond that. See? And from there, the mountains are straight ahead. Aim for those and you'll see a big waterfall. That's where the caves begin.'

I couldn't photograph the map because my phone battery was dead, so I did a quick sketch in my notebook instead. Then I picked up the backpack and clicked my fingers at Gasket. Time to go. I walked over to the door – and stopped with my hand on the handle.

'When I . . . get kidnapped, will the guards come soon?'

Mr Nyx nodded reassuringly. 'The moment I give the signal. Don't worry. They'll race to the mountains – and *destroy* the People of the Leaf!'

He grinned and gave me a thumbs up. Then

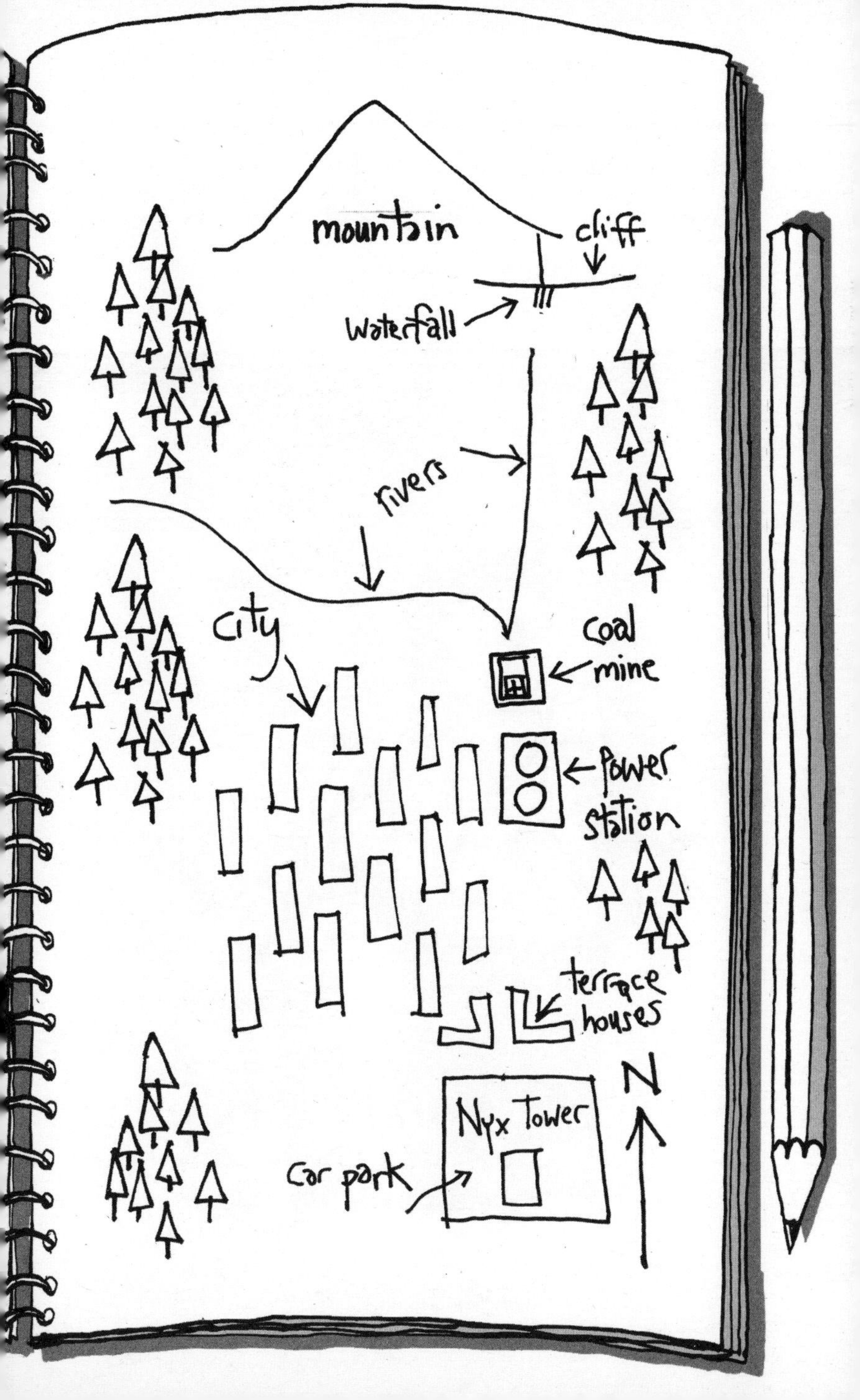

mountain

cliff

Waterfall →

rivers →

← coal mine

← power station

city

terrace houses

Nyx Tower

Car park →

N ↑

Selina led the way back to the lift. Two minutes later, Gasket and I were walking out of the factory – ready to start our secret mission.

## Chapter 15
## The Climber on the Tower

I'd forgotten about the fog.

Up in Mr Nyx's office, I'd got used to bright sunlight and clear blue sky. But the moment I walked out of the factory, I was back in the dirty, choking fog. How was I going to find the mountains? I couldn't even see where the quad bike was.

But Gasket knew. He gave me a puzzled look that said, *Why are we standing still?* Then he tugged at the edge of my jacket, pulling me across the car park.

'OK,' I said. 'I'll follow you.'

He headed into the fog, trotting right to the edge of the car park – and there was the bike, just where I'd left it. Gasket sat and looked up at me, as if he was saying, *What now?*

'Now we go and rescue Aunt Caz!' I said out loud.

I climbed on to the bike and he jumped up beside me. I switched on the engine and had another look at the map I'd sketched in my notebook. Then we set off, heading back past the factory. Weaving our way between rows of dirty old cars and motorbikes.

When we finally reached the far side of the car park, I peered into the fog, looking for the alley Mr Nyx had told me to follow. For a second I couldn't see anything. Then I spotted it, running between two rows of houses.

It was very narrow. For most of the way, the houses were all the same – small red brick terraces, with grimy walls. But suddenly I came to a wide, empty square. In the centre was a huge white pillar, disappearing up into the smog.

*That must be the bottom of one of the towers*, I thought. *That's why it hasn't got any windows down here.*

I was going to ride straight past, when I suddenly noticed something odd. A movement, halfway up the pillar. I slowed down, glancing sideways to try and see what it was. It looked almost as if there was someone climbing up the outside of the tower. But why would anyone . . . ?

'**EEECH!**' yelled a voice in front of me.

I jammed on the brakes, so fast I almost fell off the bike.

It was a girl, around my own age. She must have stepped into the road without looking – just as I turned to stare at the tower. Thank goodness I'd been going slowly! I jumped off the bike, to make sure she was OK.

She didn't look hurt – but she was furious! As I came towards her, she spat out a long string of fierce, angry words. I didn't understand any of them, but I knew exactly what she meant.

And she was absolutely right.

'I'm sorry,' I said. 'I'm *really sorry*. I should have been watching. I promise I'll be more careful. I just –'

She was still shouting, all the time I was speaking. And then, suddenly – she wasn't. She stopped in the middle of what she was saying and took a step towards me. Gasket froze, growling in the back of his throat.

The girl stared at me for a moment and then – smiled. In quite a different voice, she said something that sounded like *grio khazat*.

I didn't know what that meant, but I didn't want to upset her again, so I said the same words back to her. '*Grio khazat*.'

That made her laugh – it must have been my accent – but it was a friendly laugh. I wished I could talk to her, but I didn't know any other words in her language. And anyway, I had to keep going, to rescue Aunt Caz. So I nodded and smiled and climbed back on to the bike.

The girl said something else, looking very serious, and wagged her finger at me.

No prizes for guessing what *that* meant!

'Yes, I will,' I said. 'I promise. I'll be really, *really* careful.'

She obviously understood. She smiled and stepped away, waving goodbye. I grinned and waved back, feeling as though I'd made a friend, even though we couldn't talk to each other. Then I got back on the bike.

Before I set off again, I had a quick look back at the tower, but there was nothing to see except bare, white walls. No sign of anyone climbing.

I must have imagined it.

97

I drove on down the alley heading towards the power station. I was humming happily to myself – until I realized why the girl had suddenly turned friendly.

*She'd spotted the leaf in my pocket.*

That meant she was one of *them*. The People of the Leaf.

*They're everywhere!* I thought. Maybe it was a good thing I didn't understand the language. I had to keep my mouth shut and my eyes open – and follow all Mr Nyx's instructions. I couldn't trust anyone.

'It's you and me against the world, Gasket!' I said.

## Chapter 16
# Dust and Smoke

When I finally reached the end of the alley, I saw a vast building ahead, with black clouds billowing out of its two huge cooling towers.

'That's the power station, Gasket,' I said. 'But why is it so dirty?'

Gasket whined and shook his head from side to side. The smoke smelled bad to me and I could see it was much worse for him, but we had to keep going.

I steered past the power station, trying to see beyond it. For a while, there was nothing but smog and more smog. Then I began to hear a distant rumbling noise – the sound of machinery moving.

'We're going the right way,' I said. 'That must be the mine.'

Before long, I felt something gritty in my mouth, and when I licked my finger it came away covered with dust. Gasket gave a sudden, sharp bark.

'You're right!' I patted his head. 'We're almost at the mine!'

As we got closer, I saw the same kind of dust coating

the ground and drifting through the air around us. The rumbling noise was directly underneath now. The sound of big machines cutting through rock.

*It's coal!* I thought. *They're mining coal. That's what the power station burns − and that's what runs the factory.* Suddenly I understood the whole system. It was like a machine all right − but it was *dirty* machinery. The cooling towers were belching out clouds of pollution. No wonder the city was covered in smog!

Soon I could see two scaffolding towers above the mine, with big wheels turning as they lifted the cage bringing the miners up from underground.

They reached the surface just as we arrived in the car park beside the shaft. The cage doors opened and a crowd of miners trudged away, looking exhausted, as though they'd worked a long shift.

The next group of miners started filing into the lift. As I rode past, one or two of them noticed my leaf and gave me a thumbs up. I nodded and smiled back, but I didn't stop. I steered the bike past them and headed for the far side of the car park, watching for the mountains in the distance.

But I couldn't see them. When I got to the end of the car park, there was nothing ahead. Not even a track. Just a wall of thick, grey smog.

*I can't go on*, I thought. *I CAN'T.*

Then Gasket nudged me with his nose, as if he was saying, *Don't waste time!*

And suddenly I remembered the jackdaws in the bedroom, and the cousins screaming, and all the soot. I'd felt the same then, but I'd made myself deal with it. And I could deal with this too.

I reached across and patted Gasket's head. 'You're right. We mustn't stay here. I can't see the mountains, but Mr Nyx said they were straight ahead – so let's go and find them!'

I squeezed on the thumb throttle and the bike picked up speed, bumping out of the car park and over the rough ground beyond. For three or four seconds, it was like riding blindfold.

And then I saw something. Away in the distance, the fog thickened into huge grey shapes, massive and solid, rising up towards the sky.

'There they are, Gasket! The mountains!'

Gasket started barking with excitement and I grinned. 'We can do it! We can get there! HERE WE COME, AUNT CAZ!'

## Chapter 17
## Look Out!

It was a long, rough ride. For the first few kilometres, there were no plants. The ground was totally bare. Just dry, crumbling earth. We bumped over rocks and thumped down into dusty hollows. My teeth rattled and my bones shook, even though I was trying to ride carefully.

After twenty minutes or so, we started seeing scattered blades of grass. At first they were pale and feeble, but gradually they got greener, and other plants began to appear. When we reached the first bush, I stopped the bike and gave Gasket some water. Then we both stared up at the mountains.

They were clearer now. The sky in front of us was still hazy, but the fog had thinned. I could feel a faint breeze and see patches of snow on the high peaks. And straight ahead – yes! – there was a fine white streak down the nearest mountainside.

'Look, Gasket!' I pointed. 'There's the waterfall! Come on – let's go!'

I wanted to drive at top speed, but the ground was stony and uneven. I couldn't risk a crash – and I'd just promised to be careful. I thought of the girl and her wagging finger and made myself slow down, even though it felt as if we'd never reach the waterfall. Because we would. All we had to do was keep going . . .

When we finally got there, it took my breath away.

The water dropped sheer, for hundreds of metres, into a wide, deep pool surrounded by reeds. There was a strong, fresh wind and I could hear birds calling. I got off the bike and sat down on a patch of grass.

Real, green grass.

Gasket flopped down beside me and we shared the rest of the food and water. I knew we'd need all our strength for the next bit of our journey.

I could have stayed there for hours – but we had to get on. We needed to reach the top of the waterfall before it started getting dark. And it was going to be a slow, difficult ride.

I stepped back from the pool and looked up.

The waterfall had cut a deep cleft in the rock. There was no way of getting up the cleft itself. Not without climbing equipment. I looked at the slopes on either side of it. The one on the left was very steep. I knew the bike wouldn't make it up there. But the slope on the right was gentler. Maybe if I zigzagged . . . ?

I climbed back on to the bike and called to Gasket. 'Come on! Let's give it a try!'

We got nearly all the way up. Then I heard the engine struggling. We'd have to climb the rest. I wedged the bike

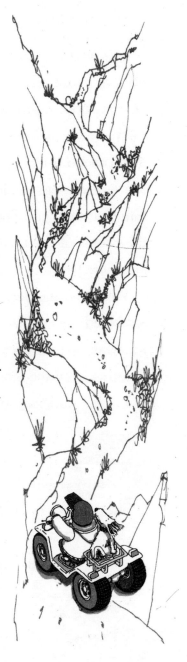

behind a tough, scraggy bush and looked round carefully, to make sure I remembered the place. Then Gasket and I scrambled up the last bit of the slope.

We made a lot of noise. Loose stones tumbled down and Gasket kept barking at rabbits. A couple of times I had to grab his collar and yell at him, to stop him chasing them. But that was all good. We wanted the People of the Leaf to hear us. Where were their lookouts?

We didn't see anyone until we reached the top. I scrabbled the last few metres, to the place where the waterfall poured over the edge, and I heard a voice shouting from the other side of the water.

I didn't understand the words, but I could see the

person who was shouting. It was a boy, about my age.

He shouted again and I yelled back, across the waterfall. 'I'm looking for my aunt! She's called Caz. Do you know where she is?'

'Caz?' the boy shouted.

'Yes! Have you seen her?'

The boy seemed to understand. But he was just pretending – to keep me looking in the wrong direction. I didn't realize until Gasket suddenly started growling.

He'd spotted the real lookouts – sneaking up behind us!

By the time I turned round, it was too late. The men were there.

They threw a sack over my head and tied my hands behind me. And they got Gasket as well. He was barking frantically now, but the sound was muffled. He was in a sack too.

'Don't worry, Gasket!' I called. Trying to sound calm. 'It's going to be all right.'

I heard the men muttering together. Then they started pulling things out of my belt.

'Don't take those!' I shouted. 'They're just tools — not weapons!'

What did they think I was going to do? Cut my way out of the sack and attack them? With my hands tied?

It was no use yelling. They unstrapped the belt and took it away. Then one of the men hoisted me over his shoulder and we started moving. I couldn't see anything, but I could tell we were climbing.

Going further up, into the mountains.

Chapter 18
Into the Caves

*I'm not a prisoner. I'm a secret agent,* I kept telling myself. This was all part of Mr Nyx's plan. We'd tricked the People of the Leaf and they were taking me to their hideout. I felt for the badge Mr Nyx had given me and held on to it, to stop myself feeling helpless.

I had to stay cool. Like Beddington Potts. The People of the Leaf were taking me to their secret hideout and I was going to rescue Aunt Caz! Once we stopped moving, there would only be a couple of hours to wait. And then the city guards would come storming in to rescue us.

*If the badge works . . .*

Of course it would! It *had* to work!

After half an hour or so, we stopped and I heard more voices. Six or seven at least. Then we moved again, into somewhere cold. The sound of the men's footsteps echoed round us, and I guessed we were in the caves.

Gasket growled inside his sack.

'Quiet, boy,' I said softly. If he started barking, the men might get annoyed with him. But the sound of his voice made me feel better, all the same. We were a team. Working together.

The men tramped on and on, as if we were going deep into the mountain. It felt like hours before they finally stopped and put us down on the hard rock floor.

And suddenly I heard a voice I knew.

'What's in those sacks? Have you *finally* brought me some paper?'

'Aunt Caz!' I yelled. 'Aunt Caz, it's me!'

'Ollie?'

As the men walked away, I heard her running towards me. She untied my hands and pulled the sack off my head. We were standing in a small, shadowy cave, with a lantern hanging from the ceiling.

'What took you so long?' she said.

I blinked up at her. 'So *long*?'

'Well, I knew you'd find me.' She beamed and patted my arm. 'You're such a clever boy. I told them to look out for you.' She looked past me, at the other sack. 'What's in there? Have you brought me some paper?'

'It's my dog,' I said.

Aunt Caz shook her head at me. 'Don't be silly, Ollie. You haven't got a dog.'

'I have now.' I undid the sack, as fast as I could, and Gasket jumped out and started licking my face. 'Why do you want paper, anyway?'

'For my book, of course,' Aunt Caz said impatiently. 'I can't send these walls to the publisher, can I?'

'The *walls*?' For the first time, I had a proper look round the cave. There were words scratched all over the walls. Lots and *lots* of words.

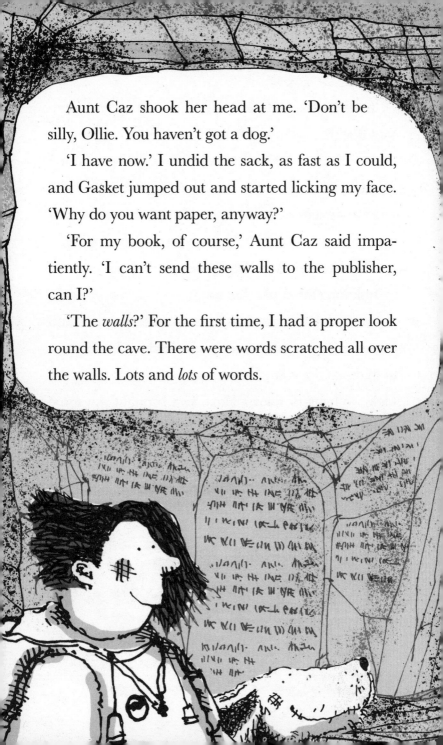

'I *had* to start writing my book,' Aunt Caz said. 'But I didn't have my notebook. Or a pen. Thank goodness I pinned up the hole in my jacket before I left home!'

I stared at her. 'You scratched all those words with a *pin*?'

'I'm a writer!' Aunt Caz waved her hands about. 'I have to get the words down!'

I shook my head. 'How could you even *think* about Beddington Potts? You're a prisoner! You've been kidnapped by a dangerous gang!'

'A dangerous gang?' Aunt Caz stared at me. 'What are you talking about?'

'Those men,' I said. I looked round, to see if they were listening, but they'd all disappeared. 'The People of the Leaf.'

'But –' For a second Aunt Caz gaped, as if she was too surprised to speak. Then she shook her head at me. 'You've got it all wrong, Ollie. The People of the Leaf are the good guys. They're *heroes*!'

Chapter 19
Doctor
Renata

Heroes? What was she talking about?

'They kidnapped you!' I said. 'Pushed you into a dustbin and carried you off to the mountains. What's good about that?'

Aunt Caz flapped her hand. 'Don't *fuss*. They had to kidnap me. When I went into that kitchen, I opened their cookery book and saw . . . something very secret. I could have ruined all their plans.'

'But – but –'

'They're really kind.' Aunt Caz patted my arm. 'When I told them about you, they offered to go back and kidnap you as well. To keep us together.'

'They offered *what*?'

She laughed. 'I told them not to bother. I knew you'd come and find me.'

I felt like shaking her. 'Aunt Caz, I came to *rescue* you!'

'I don't need rescuing.' Aunt Caz pulled the pin out of her jacket and went across to the cave wall. 'What I need is *paper*. Oh – and a bit of help with that mini-drone.'

'*What*?'

'The mini-drone you showed me. In the turnip café.' Aunt Caz shook her head impatiently.

'You mean this?' I took it out of my pocket.

'Of course I mean that!' She came across and poked it. 'You said Beddington Potts should have one, but you didn't *explain*. How does he control it?'

I shrugged. 'I use my phone.'

'Show me! I need to see it working.'

I shook my head. 'Sorry, my battery's dead. And anyway –'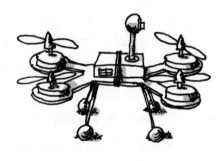

*Anyway, it won't work down here*, I was going to say. But Aunt Caz didn't give me time to finish.

'Get your phone charged then! Go and see Dr Renata!'

'A doctor?' What was she talking about? 'I'm not ill –'

Aunt Caz sighed. 'I haven't got time to explain. Just go and see Dr Renata, Ollie. She'll tell you everything. Go on down the tunnel and take the first right.' She turned away and started scratching words on the wall.

'But –'

'Go *on*, Ollie! I need to finish this chapter.' She started scratching faster. 'I've thought of something really clever for Beddington Potts to do with that drone . . . '

It was no use trying to talk to her now. *Might as well*

*go and find this Dr Renata*, I thought. At least I'd get my phone charged. And I hadn't got anything else to do for the next two hours.

'Come on, Gasket,' I said. 'Let's do it.'

I left the cave, took a couple of steps along the tunnel – and bumped into the side.

Once we were out of the cave, it was pitch-dark. There were no lights in the tunnel and it climbed steeply, twisting and turning. I went very slowly, keeping one hand on the wall.

Gasket was right beside me. He kept nudging my arm, as if he wanted me to go faster. But how could I?

'It's too dark,' I said. 'I'll trip.'

He nudged again, impatiently, and I started getting annoyed.

'Don't be so bossy!' I muttered.

It was all right for him! He could see in the dark much better than I could. I caught hold of his collar and walked as fast as I dared, still running my hand along the wall so we didn't miss the right turn.

'Here!' I said, when we reached it.

As we turned, I saw a gleam of light ahead – and Gasket pulled himself free, racing towards it. I jogged after him, as fast as I could without falling over. We came out into a big cave, lit by dozens of lanterns.

With paper everywhere.

There were long scrolls of paper, hanging from stalactites, draped over stalagmites and spread out across the floor. *I'll get some for Aunt Caz!* I thought.

But then I realized it was no good for her. Every single piece of paper was covered in diagrams. On both sides. What were they doing there?

Before I could have a proper look, a voice spoke from the far side of the cave.

'Hello?'

I turned round and saw a woman in overalls, sitting on a rock. Gasket started towards her and I grabbed hold of his collar again.

'I'm Ollie,' I said. 'I – um – I'm looking for Dr Renata.'

She nodded. 'I'm Dr Renata. What can I do for you?'

'I'm not *ill*,' I said quickly.

'Glad to hear it.' She gave another brisk nod. 'I'm no good at fixing people. Only machines.'

'*Machines?*'

'I'm a Doctor of Engineering.'

She was an *engineer*? For a second, I was too surprised to speak. Gasket nudged my hand again, as if he was saying, *Get on with it!*

'I – Aunt Caz said you could charge my phone,' I muttered.

Dr Renata gave me a sharp look. 'Yes, I can. I've got a battery here – but you won't get a signal in the caves. Or anywhere on the mountains.'

'I don't need a signal. It's for my drone. Aunt Caz wants to see how it works.' I took it out to show her.

Very carefully, Dr Renata lifted the tiny drone out of my hand. 'Did you *make* this?'

I nodded. 'For my jackdaw scarer. To fly at them if they land on the chimney.'

Dr Renata laughed. 'It looks as though you're an engineer too. Want to have a look at my diagrams while your phone's charging?'

She held out her hand and I gave her the phone. Then I looked round at the pieces of paper. 'Did *you* draw all these diagrams?'

'Of course.' Dr Renata plugged in the phone. Then she stood up and led me across the cave. 'Start with this one.'

I went to stand beside her. 'It looks like a sort of

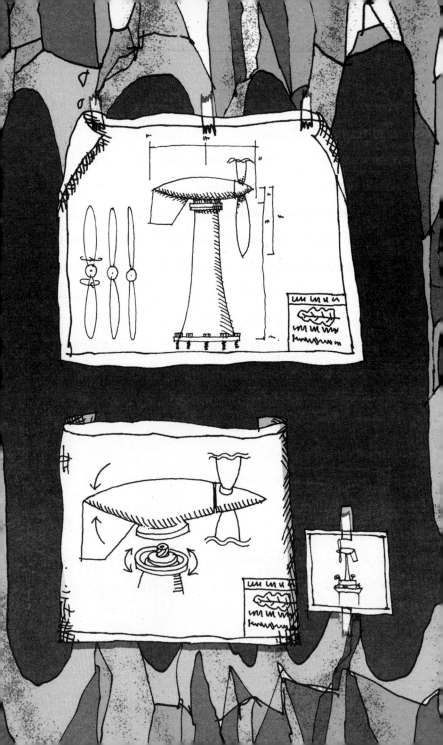

wind turbine. Only I can't see how . . .'

'Try the next diagram.' Dr Renata pointed. 'And then the one over there. That shows the wind flow. And then . . .'

She led me round the cave. The diagrams were clear and detailed – and beautiful! By the time I reached the last one, I was almost too excited to breathe.

Dr Renata had designed a new, superefficient wind turbine. A perfect machine.

'Like it?' she said, when I got to the last diagram.

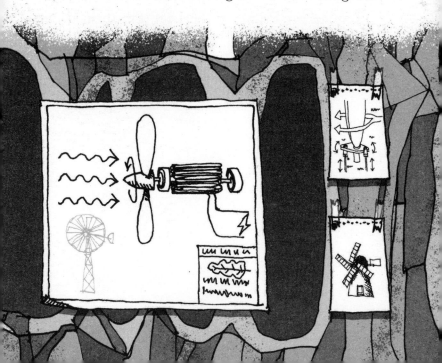

I nodded, trying to find the right words. 'It's . . .
genius! You have to get out of here – so you can build
lots of them!'

'Get out of here?' Dr Renata stared at me. 'What
do you mean?'

Wasn't that obvious? 'You have to get away from
the People of the Leaf! I don't know why they kidnapped you, but –'

'You've got it all wrong!' Dr Renata shook her
head. 'Nobody's kidnapped me.'

I didn't understand. 'So – why are you down here?'

'I *started* the People of the Leaf. I'm their leader,
Ollie.'

## Chapter 20
# The People of the Leaf

I was too surprised to speak. I just stared at her, with my mouth open.

Dr Renata waved her hand at the diagrams. 'That's why I designed the wind turbine. Didn't your aunt explain?'

I shook my head. 'She just said I should talk to you.'

'Right.' Dr Renata took a deep breath. 'OK, I need to show you something. But take care.

It's a bit of a scramble.'

Before I could say anything, she was off, into another tunnel on the far side of the cave. Gasket whined anxiously.

I felt anxious too. Were we moving around too much? The guards wouldn't come until we'd been in the same place for two hours. Maybe we should have stayed with Aunt Caz.

But I needed to understand about the wind turbine.

'Come on, Gasket. We have to find out what's going on.'

As soon as I walked into the tunnel, I realized it went up almost vertically. I waved Gasket in front of me, in case he needed a push, and we followed Dr Renata, scrambling from one rocky ledge to another. On and on and on.

At last, I saw light at the top. And Dr Renata's face peering down at me.

'Nearly there!' she called.

I gave Gasket one last shove and he scrambled through the opening. When he was out, he bent over so I could catch hold of his collar. Then he backed away, pulling me out too – and there we were, out in the light, at the very top of the mountain.

I could see a steep slope falling away in front of us, with a cloud of spray – where the waterfall tumbled over the cliff. Beyond that, in the valley below, was the city where we'd left the van.

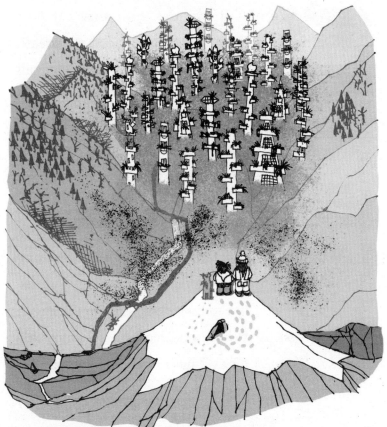

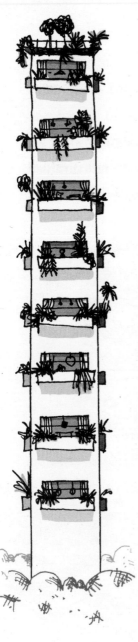

But I couldn't see the van. Or the factory, or the mine, or the rows of dirty little terraced houses. They were all hidden by thick, horrible smog. You wouldn't have known the city was there at all.

Except for the towers.

It was the third time I'd seen them, but they still took my breath away, because they were so tall and beautiful. And *clean*. Their silvery-white walls glittered in the sunlight and even from that distance I could make out the plants growing on the balconies.

'Lovely, aren't they?' Dr Renata said softly. 'It's a pity they all belong to a few rich people. Everyone else has to live down there in the smog. Where nothing grows except turnips. That's why I founded the

People of the Leaf.'

I swallowed nervously. 'To take over the city?' I said. 'So *you* can live in the towers?'

'What?' For a moment, Dr Renata looked startled. Then she laughed. 'No, of course not! We just want to get rid of the smog. That's why I designed the wind turbines.'

I looked down at the smog, thinking about the mine and the power station and the Groundlings' grimy houses – and suddenly I understood! Dr Renata's plan was simple and life-changing. A real engineer's plan.

'You mean – the city won't need to burn coal any more? Because you'll be using wind energy.'

She nodded. 'Clean, green electricity for everyone! People don't *have* to live with terrible pollution. I explained it all to the city council, ten years ago. But they didn't want to know.'

'So then you founded the People of the Leaf?' I said.

'I had to do something!' Dr Renata said fiercely.

'So I started looking for other people who thought like me. People who knew the city *had* to change. And we've been planning WT Day ever since.'

'WT –?' Then I got it. 'Wind Turbine Day!'

Dr Renata nodded again. 'Ten years of planning – and now we're almost there. Only a week to go!'

'Then what?'

She grinned. 'Next Monday, we'll march into the city – without any warning – and fit wind turbines on top of all those lovely white towers. Then we'll close the coal mine, for ever.'

Everything suddenly started making sense. 'Is that why you kidnapped Aunt Caz? Because she found out about WT Day?'

Dr Renata sighed. 'She saw the date. If she'd told other people, she'd have ruined everything. Our plan won't work unless it's a surprise.'

'Well now it will be.' I looked down at the towers again, imagining the city as it could be. As it *would* be, if Dr Renata's plans succeeded. 'A really *good* surprise.'

'Good for most people.' Dr Renata pulled a face. 'But there's one man who's going to be furious. He's done everything he can to stop us.'

My heart gave a terrible thud. I'd been so busy thinking about the wind turbines I'd forgotten about being a secret agent. 'One person –?'

'The man who's made a fortune out of coal,' Dr Renata said bitterly. 'The man who thinks our city belongs to him – Mr Erebus Nyx!'

## Chapter 21
## Which Side Are You On?

Erebus Nyx? But . . . but . . .

For a second, I couldn't speak. I just stared at Dr Renata, with words swirling round in my head.

*This is a well-run, successful city . . .*

*. . . we just want to get rid of the smog . . .*

*. . . the Groundlings choose to live lower down . . .*

*. . . people don't have to live with terrible pollution . . .*

*. . . the People of the Leaf . . . are plotting to take over . . .*

*. . . the man who thinks our city belongs to him . . .*

I had to decide who was right. But how could I? I wasn't like Beddington Potts – sharper than a needle. I was just Ollie Spark. All on my own, with no one to tell me what to think.

I'd have to work it out for myself.

I sat down on a rock and closed my eyes. Gasket laid his head on my knee and I stroked his ears and thought about Dr Renata and Mr Nyx. About the wind turbines and the smog. The white towers, with their balconies full of fruit and vegetables . . . and

Groundlings who lived on turnips. I remembered Erebus Nyx's beautiful office, and the tired miners finishing their shift. And the girl who had jumped in front of my bike. Gradually, things started fitting together, like the parts of a machine.

I took a deep breath and opened my eyes.

Dr Renata was watching me. 'Are you all right, Ollie?'

'I have to tell you something,' I said slowly. 'Before I came here, I talked to Erebus Nyx. He told me the People of the Leaf were planning to ruin the city.'

Dr Renata was very quiet for a moment. Then she said, 'Do you know why we're called the People of the Leaf?'

I shook my head.

'Come over here. I want to show you some-thing.' She beckoned me across to the far side of the mountaintop.

From there, we looked down into a little valley. At the top of the valley we could see a small clump of trees.

They weren't dead!

Their trunks were straight and strong, with smooth grey bark. Their leaves were a bright, fresh green, healthy and flourishing. Drawing in sunlight and taking carbon dioxide out of the air – like perfect, living machines. Just seeing them made me smile.

'When I was a child,' Dr Renata said, 'those trees grew all over this mountain. Lovely, tall trees with leaves that opened at the very start of spring and golden flowers in the summer. But pollution from the smog has killed all the others. These are the only ones left. Soon they'll be dead too – unless we fit the wind turbines and get rid of the pollution.'

'That's why their leaf is your symbol?' I said.

Dr Renata nodded. 'The precious, beautiful grio leaf.'

'Grio?' That word again. 'Like . . . *grio khazat*?'

'Just like that.' Dr Renata stared down at the trees. 'It's our password. *I choose the leaf.*'

*I choose* . . . I had to choose too. Who was I going to believe? Doctor Renata. Or Mr Nyx? It was time to decide. I stared down at the grio trees, and the smog below them.

And I knew what I had to do.

Slowly I unpinned the blue badge from my jacket. I held it out to Dr Renata. 'Mr Nyx gave me this badge. It's got a microchip, so he can track me and find your headquarters. He guessed you would bring me here. When I've been in the same place for two hours – he'll send in the city guards.'

Dr Renata took the badge and turned it over in

141

her hand. For a moment, she was very quiet. Then she looked at her big, old-fashioned watch. 'You've only been here about an hour. We've still got a bit of time.'

'I'll go,' I said. 'I've got a quad bike near the waterfall. I'll take the badge and ride as far away as I can – until the fuel runs out.'

Dr Renata shook her head. 'I can't let you do that. And anyway –' she grinned suddenly – 'I've got a *much* better idea. Let's go and find Hamish.'

## Chapter 22
## Turnips for Supper

Dr Renata jumped up and started back down the vertical tunnel. I followed her, hanging on to Gasket's collar, to stop him slithering down too fast. The big metal studs on the collar hurt my hand, but I didn't let go.

*At least Mr Nyx gave me one useful thing*, I thought.

By the time we reached the bottom, Dr Renata was racing across the cave, with a torch in her hand. I followed her – snatching up my phone as I went

– and we ran back past Aunt Caz and along another tunnel. Dr Renata was shouting as she ran.

'Hamish! I've got a job for you! Put your running shoes on!'

We came out of the tunnels, into a grassy space at the entrance to the caves. There were half a dozen people sitting on the ground out there. Dr Renata ran across to one of them – a small, wiry man who

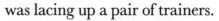 was lacing up a pair of trainers.

She pushed the badge into his hand. 'Take this . . . to Grey Tor!' she panted. 'Drop it . . . into the biggest bog . . . you can find!'

Hamish didn't ask any questions. He just nodded, pinned the badge to his shirt, and raced away over the mountain. Dr Renata smiled as she watched him go.

'He's a champion fell runner,' she said. 'It's getting dark, but he knows Grey Tor like the back of his hand. I don't envy the city guards when they get stuck in those bogs.'

'I'm really sorry –' I started to say.

Dr Renata held up her hand to stop me. 'Don't worry. Erebus Nyx is always making plans to destroy us. But so far, we've always kept one step ahead. Now come and have supper.'

I realized I was really, *REALLY* hungry. 'What's for supper?' I said.

Dr Renata pulled a face. 'Guess!'

'Turnips?'

'Turnip soup!' She grinned. 'Let's go and fetch your Aunt Caz.'

Gasket barked, as if he agreed with her, and Dr Renata laughed.

'He's a great dog. How old is he?'

'I don't know,' I said. 'I just found him this morning. Trapped inside a roundabout. I think he was a stray.'

'Someone must care about him,' Dr Renata said. 'He's wearing a brand-new collar.'

I frowned. 'Don't all dogs have to wear collars? I

thought that was one of the city regulations.'

'No?' Dr Renata sounded puzzled. 'Whatever makes you think that?'

'It's –'

*It's what Erebus Nyx said.*

I nearly blurted it out. But suddenly I thought of Beddington Potts and all his secret spying devices. What had Aunt Caz said? . . . *lots of special gadgets, like . . . a secret camera . . . and a hidden microphone . . .*

I looked down at the collar. *No!* I thought. *NOOOO!!!!* But my mind drowned that out with a huge, horrified *YES!!!*

I'd been tricked! I mustn't say anything – not another word – until I had a safe way to tell Dr Renata. And there was only one way I could think of . . .

I turned and raced back into the caves, with Gasket close behind me. I heard Dr Renata calling – 'Ollie? What's the matter?' – but I didn't answer. I didn't look back. I just hoped she would follow me through the tunnels. To Aunt Caz's cave.

Chapter 23
Emergency!

By the time I got there, I was out of breath. I raced into the cave, right behind Gasket, and Aunt Caz looked round from the wall.

'Oh there you are, Ollie. Did you find Dr Renata?'

I nodded and looked back. Dr Renata was just coming into the cave. I turned towards her – facing away from Gasket – and put a finger to my lips. *Don't speak! Please don't speak, Dr Renata!*

Dr Renata raised her eyebrows, as if she was

asking a question, but she understood what I meant. She didn't make a sound.

I turned back to Aunt Caz. She was staring at us both, looking puzzled. I put my finger to my lips again and then pointed at the pin she was holding. Reluctantly, she handed it over and I found a clean piece of wall. Quickly I scratched some words.

EREBUS NYX GAVE ME THAT COLLAR FOR GASKET

'What –?' Aunt Caz started.

Dr Renata laid a hand on her arm, before she could say anything else. She read what I'd written and then took the pin and scratched some words of her own.

KEEP TALKING WHILE I TAKE A LOOK

I nodded and turned to Aunt Caz. 'It's turnip soup for supper,' I said. 'That might be another good recipe for Beddington Potts. Do you think he likes turnips?'

Out of the corner of my eye, I could see Dr Renata patting Gasket's head, very gently, while she looked

at the collar.

Aunt Caz looked baffled for a moment – and then she realized something exciting was going on. Her eyes gleamed and she started talking very fast, about turnip recipes, waving her hands around and chanting lists of spices.

'Nigella seed and star anise, paprika and chilli and tamarind, caraway and cassia bark . . .'

She was still chanting when Dr Renata went back to the wall and started scratching again.

THE MIDDLE STUD'S A MIC

My guess was right. Erebus Nyx had fooled me. He'd been listening to everything, ever since I left his office. He wasn't really interested in rescuing Aunt Caz – he just wanted to discover Dr Renata's plans. And now he had.

And he knew WT Day was next Monday.

Dr Renata turned round, looking stunned and miserable. *She's spent ten years planning*, I thought, *and it's all ruined. If she doesn't cancel WT Day, the city guards will be there on Monday. Waiting to arrest everyone.*

And it was all my fault. For trusting Erebus Nyx.

How could I have been so stupid? How could I have trusted him, just because he said I was brave and promised to help me? I felt like crawling into the furthest, darkest tunnel I could find and hiding away for ever.

Then Gasket came padding across the cave. He licked my hand and looked up at me. Gave me a little nudge with his nose, as if he was waiting for me to do something. But what *could* I do? Dr Renata's plan was wrecked and there was no way to save it now.

*Unless . . .*

Suddenly, my brain started working again. Maybe . . . maybe if Dr Renata acted fast . . .

I turned round and took the pin out of her hand. As fast as I could, I scratched on the wall again.

*WHY DO YOU HAVE TO WAIT FOR MONDAY?*

*FIT THE TURBINES NOW!!!*

Dr Renata looked over my shoulder, reading the words as I scratched them. She gave a sad little smile and started shaking her head, as if moving WT Day was impossible.

And then she stopped.

She looked back at the wall, read the words again, and frowned, as if she was thinking hard. Suddenly, she gave a brisk little nod.

'Let's go and have supper!' she said brightly.

Beckoning to me and Aunt Caz, she set off along the tunnel opposite. Aunt Caz hurried after her, still reciting the names of spices, as if she was casting a spell.

'Cardamom and cumin and nutmeg! Turmeric and ras-el-hanout! Sumac and harissa and grains of paradise . . . !'

I had no idea what was happening, but Gasket had pricked up his ears. He started tugging at my sleeve, to make me follow Dr Renata.

Why was he so excited?

'OK,' I said. 'Let's go and have some lovely turnip soup!'

We followed Dr Renata and Aunt Caz along the corridor and came out into a cave full of people. An old man was doling out mugs of soup and a dozen other people were sitting round on stools, eating and chatting.

'That smells good!' Dr Renata said cheerfully. 'I hope there's some left for us.'

The old man nodded. As he reached for more mugs, Dr Renata bent down and unstrapped Gasket's collar. She put her finger to her lips and then pointed at Aunt Caz's wrist.

Aunt Caz held out her arm. Dr Renata put the

collar on, like a bracelet, and then waved at a spare stool.

'Here's Caz!' she said to everyone else. 'If you ask her nicely, she might tell you a story.'

She waited for a moment, to make sure Aunt Caz was settled. Then she beckoned to me and Gasket – and led us out of the cave again, very quickly.

What was going on?

There was only one way to find out. Gasket and I followed Dr Renata, as fast as we could.

Chapter 24
I Can
Do That!

As soon as we were clear of the upper cave, Dr Renata started talking.

'You're right, Ollie. We have to move *NOW*. It's our only hope. If we can start fitting the turbines at midnight, the people in the towers won't see us. We can get them all into place before Erebus Nyx realizes what's happening. The only problem . . . ' She frowned.

'What is it?' I said.

Dr Renata sighed. 'Somehow, I have to tell our people in the city. And get the turbine parts delivered in time.'

'Can't you just . . . phone? There must be a signal down in the city.'

Dr Renata smiled bitterly. 'Oh, there's a signal all right. And Erebus Nyx would love it if we used our phones!'

I didn't understand. 'What do you mean?'

'He's got spies monitoring the phone network – so our people never answer their phones. If they did, Erebus Nyx would have found out our plans long ago.' Dr Renata stopped to think. 'No, I'll have to send a messenger. But that means explaining to someone – and the time's ticking away.'

'I could go,' I said. 'But I can't run as fast as Hamish. If only I had my quad bike!'

Dr Renata turned to look at me. 'But you have!'

'What?'

She didn't explain. Just turned left, into another tunnel, beckoning me to follow her. After a few moments, we came out into yet another cave. And there, in the middle of it, was . . .

The quad bike! With my toolbelt lying on the seat!

I was amazed. 'How did they get down here?'

'The lookouts brought them in,' Doctor Renata said. 'We were going to give them back – once we'd checked you were on our side.'

I ran across and snatched up the belt. 'Of course I'm on your side!' I said, as I strapped it on. 'Just tell me what I can do!'

'Do you think . . .' Dr Renata hesitated for a moment. 'Could you ride the bike through these tunnels?'

'Through the *tunnels*?' I thought about it. 'I don't see why not. As long as they're wide enough. But why –?'

She crossed the cave, to another opening. 'That tunnel connects to the old mine workings – where the wind turbine parts are stored. Our plan won't work unless the miners can bring them up in time. We have to make sure they can do it.'

'So – you want me to go and find out?'

Dr Renata nodded. 'Will you do that for us? While I stay and explain to the people here.'

I stared at the tunnel. It looked very dark. And narrow.

'I promise it's wide enough,' Dr Renata said. 'All the way to the mine.'

She ought to know. She was an engineer.

'All right. I'll go,' I said. 'But . . . will they understand me?'

'I'll write it down.' Dr Renata pulled a notebook out of her pocket, scribbled on one of the pages and tore it out. 'Take this. Ask for Lenny. Give it to him and bring back his answer.'

I nodded.

'And −' Dr Renata hesitated for a moment. 'Have you got your phone?'

I nodded again. 'Yes, I have. But it's OK. I promise not to use it.'

'That's good. Except . . .' She took a long breath. 'If anything goes wrong − if Erebus Nyx catches you − then you *must* phone, so we can come and rescue you.'

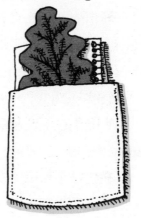

She scribbled a phone number on the bottom of her note. I took it and tucked it into my pocket, behind the leaf. 'Come on, Gasket!' I said. 'Let's go!'

Gasket gave one excited bark as we jumped on to the bike. I started the engine and turned on the headlight.

'Ride safely,' Dr Renata said. 'But *hurry*. You *must*

find Lenny before midnight.'

I nodded. 'Don't worry. We'll get there.'

Then we were off, heading into the tunnel on the far side of the cave.

For the first hundred metres or so, it was fine. The tunnel was wide and straight and its floor was smooth. The bike picked up speed and I thought, *This is easy.*

But after the first bend, everything changed. The sides closed in and there were rocks scattered over the ground. The tunnel began to twist and turn. Left . . . right . . . left . . . left . . . right.

We had to slow down and I felt the minutes ticking away. Gasket barked, as if he was saying, *Go faster!*

'I can't,' I said. 'But don't worry. We'll be there before midnight.'

And then the headlight went out.

## Chapter 25
# Racing into the Dark

I knew straight away what had happened. The bulb had gone – and there wasn't a spare.

We were alone in the dark. Deep underground.

I tried riding on, very slowly, but almost at once the front of the bike scraped against the rocks on one side. It wasn't safe to keep going like that. There was only one thing we could do.

'Come on, Gasket,' I said. 'We'll have to walk.'

I wasn't sure how. It was so dark I couldn't see

anything at all. I'd have to *feel* my way to the mine, and that would take ages. We couldn't go back. That would ruin everything. But we had to *hurry*.

I needed to reach the mine and find Lenny. By midnight.

Gasket gave another loud, excited bark, as if he was saying, 'Let's *go*!' He jumped down and I climbed off the bike, dropping the keys into my pocket. When I turned round, to start walking – Gasket wasn't there. I could hear him way down the tunnel, racing ahead of me.

For a second I was really annoyed – and then I remembered. He could see in the dark – much better than I could!

'Gasket! Here!' I shouted. He came bounding back, barking cheerfully. As if he was asking what made me so slow.

'You need to help me, Gasket,' I said. 'So we can get there in time.'

I unstrapped my tool belt and dumped the tools into the quad bike carrier. Then I looped one end of the belt round Gasket's neck, like a collar, and held on to the other end.

'OK!' I shouted. 'Let's go!'

Gasket took off like a Formula One car, dragging me along behind. I couldn't see anything and I didn't have time to think. I just had to trust him – and keep running. Sometimes I bumped against the tunnel wall, when he swung round a corner, but I hardly noticed that. All I could think about was taking Dr Renata's note to the miners.

How much time had we got? How long was it till midnight?

It was hot in the tunnel. I could hear Gasket panting and a couple of times I had to stop and catch my breath. After the first few minutes, I couldn't tell how long we'd been running, or how

much further we had to go. I couldn't think about anything except putting one foot in front of the other. Left – right – left – right . . .

The tunnels were shored up with ancient wooden pit props and I could hear the wood creaking as we went by. What would happen if one of the props gave way? I kept a tight hold on Gasket's makeshift lead and tried not to think about that. I had to keep running, keep running, keep running . . .

Gasket stopped suddenly.

I almost fell over him. 'What . . . are you . . . doing?' I gasped, trying to catch my breath. 'We have to . . . keep going.'

My voice echoed around us. We weren't in a narrow tunnel any more. We were in some kind of wide, high space. A huge cave.

Gasket had stopped because he didn't know which way to go.

Nor did I.

I sat down on the stony floor of the tunnel and Gasket put his head on my knees. Suddenly, everything looked hopeless. I was exhausted. And didn't know what time it was. Or where I needed to go. Or how to find the miners. Or . . .

I felt like giving up.

Then I remembered something Dad once said when I couldn't see how to mend our boiler. *You may not be able to fix everything, Ollie. But you must always give it your best shot.*

I wasn't finished yet. Gathering all the energy I had left, I dragged myself back to my feet. 'Come on, Gasket,' I said. 'We have to keep going. Let's feel our way round the side of the cave.'

Gasket gave a little whine, but he stood up too. And that was when I heard them. Voices – somewhere ahead of us!

I took a deep breath and shouted, with all the energy I had left. 'Help! Please help us! Help!'

For a moment, I thought no one had heard. Then the tunnel began to echo with the noise of feet running. Lots of feet. Half a dozen lights swept round a bend in front of me, shining into the cave, and I saw it for the first time. It was even bigger than I'd thought.

And it was full of turbine parts.

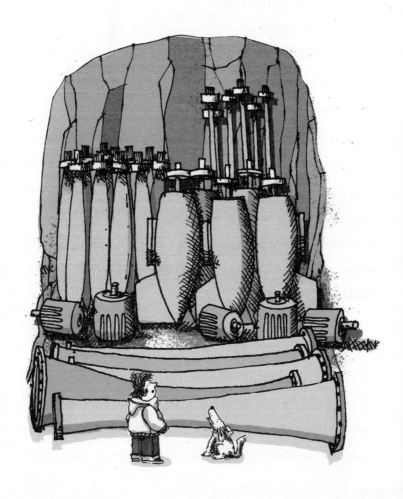

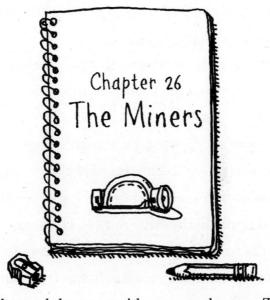

Chapter 26
The Miners

I stared round the cave, with my mouth open. There were hundreds of parts. Generators. Gearboxes. Brakes and shafts. Blades and rotors and hubs. All stacked neatly, in order. Enough to put wind turbines on top of all the towers in the city.

But how were they going to get up there?

There was no chance to think about that. People were crowding round me – miners, with lights in their helmets and faces covered in dust. They were all talking at once. It was like being back at home.

Except I couldn't understand a word they were saying.

I took a deep breath and shouted, 'Lenny!'

A big man pushed his way to the front.

'Lenny?' I said.

He nodded. I pulled Dr Renata's note out of my pocket and gave it to him. He read it carefully, looked surprised, and read it again. Then he nodded and turned round to the other miners. He started talking very fast, pointing to one person after another – and they all started moving. It was like watching a machine go into action.

Some of them ran up tunnels on the opposite side of the cave. In a few seconds, I heard the sound of engines running and the next moment long lines of trucks were coming out of every tunnel opening.

By the time the drivers put on the brakes, the other miners were ready to load up the turbine parts. They moved unbelievably fast, as if they all knew exactly what to do. And as each line of trucks was driven away, a new one took its place.

Lenny turned and said something to me. It sounded important, but I couldn't understand.

I shook my head. 'Sorry.'

He picked a piece of coal off the floor, took Dr

Renata's note out of his pocket and scribbled something on the back. Folding it in half, he pressed it into my hand.

'Dr Renata!' he said. Pointing back into the tunnel I'd come from.

I thought about going back through that tunnel. Walking all the way. It was going to take a very long time.

'I need a light,' I said.

I could see Lenny didn't understand, so I said it again.

'A *light*.' I pointed at the tunnel, shut my eyes and fumbled around with my hands – as if I couldn't see. Then I pointed up at the light on his helmet.

For a second he looked baffled. Then he laughed. He took off his helmet and strapped it on to my head. It was too big, but that didn't matter. Now I had a light, I could ride the bike when we reached it. I grinned at Lenny, and he shook my hand and clapped me on the back.

I checked Gasket's lead, to make sure it wasn't too tight, and then we set off, running back the way we'd come. Racing as fast as we could, to reach the quad bike and get the message to Dr Renata.

## Chapter 27
## Tricking the Mic

*Suppose the bike's gone?* I couldn't help worrying as we ran. *Suppose it doesn't start? Suppose the light on the helmet goes out . . . ?*

But it was all right. The bike was there. Gasket and I jumped on and it started first go. We roared back through the tunnel and into the cave we'd started from.

Dr Renata was waiting for me.

'Did you find Lenny?' she said. Very fast, before

I'd even stopped.

I nodded and switched off the bike. 'Here's his answer.'

She read it, and gave a huge grin. 'He says he can do it! He'll get all the turbine parts up to the surface in time.'

'In time for what?'

Dr Renata pushed Lenny's note into her pocket. 'In time for us to get all the turbines in place by sunrise. Before Erebus Nyx knows it's happening!'

'By *sunrise?*' Was that possible? 'But . . . who's going to do all the work?'

'Everyone!' Dr Renata said. 'All the ordinary people in the city. They've spent the last five years learning how to assemble the turbines and climb the towers.'

'So I *did* see a climber on one of the towers!' Suddenly I remembered. 'I thought I'd imagined it.'

'You *saw* someone?' Dr Renata frowned. 'They're supposed to have lookouts, to make sure no one's watching.'

'There was a girl. She jumped out in front of my bike. Did she do it on purpose, to distract me?'

Dr Renata nodded. 'Everyone's been helping, even the kids. And they're all ready. They're just waiting for the signal to start.'

'And Erebus Nyx doesn't know?' I said. 'His mic hasn't picked up anything?'

'Oh, it's picked up *lots*.' Dr Renata grinned suddenly. 'But nothing to make him suspicious. Your Aunt Caz has taken care of that!'

'Aunt *Caz*?'

'Come and see!' Dr Renata set off through the tunnels, almost running, and I hurried after her, with Gasket close behind.

Before we'd even reached the cave, I heard Aunt Caz's voice, booming ahead of us.

'. . . so Beddington Potts jumped into his super-charged car and raced after the spies, screeching round hairpin bends, all the way up the mountain. When they got to the top . . .'

'What on earth –?' I started to say. Dr Renata turned round and shook her head, putting a finger to her lips.

So the mic was in there with Aunt Caz. But what was she doing? She sounded hoarse, as though she'd been talking for hours.

We came round the corner, into the cave, and she gave us a little wave. But her voice didn't stop.

'. . . the spies jumped out of their car and scrambled into a helicopter.' She was reading the words she'd scratched on the cave walls. 'As it took off, Beddington Potts could see them laughing at him.

They thought they'd escaped. But . . .' She paused dramatically.

'But *what*?' said Dr Renata. As though she'd been listening to the whole story. 'What happened then?'

Aunt Caz gave a triumphant grin and went on, in her storytelling voice. 'Beddington Potts launched his mini-drone. Controlling it with his phone, he steered it on to the roof of the helicopter and it stayed there . . . um . . .' She looked at me.

'Maybe it had magnets?' I whispered.

Aunt Caz beamed and nodded. 'It held on *magnetically*!' she said with a flourish. 'Now Beddington Potts could track the helicopter wherever it went!'

Dr Renata held up her watch, to show her it was one o'clock in the morning. Aunt Caz grinned and gave a loud, noisy yawn.

'OK, people, that's it for tonight. Come back

tomorrow morning and I'll tell you the rest. But I need to get to bed now. And so does Ollie.'

She gave another loud yawn, took Gasket's collar off her wrist and put it on a rocky ledge in the corner of the cave. Then she said, 'Goodnight, Ollie,' in a sleepy voice.

'Goodnight, Aunt Caz.' I tried to sound sleepy too. 'Goodnight, Gasket.'

Gasket looked up at me with his head on one side. As if he was saying, *Going to bed? When there's work to do?* I smiled and patted his head, to let him know everything was OK.

Dr Renata was already on her way out of the cave.

Aunt Caz hurried after her. 'Where are you going?' she whispered.

'Down to the city,' Dr Renata muttered, without stopping. 'I've sent messengers already, to wake people up. Now I need to go myself – to tell them *grio is go!*'

'Take us too!' hissed Aunt Caz.

Dr Renata turned round, looking surprised. 'You?'

'We're with you all the way!' Aunt Caz punched the air 'And it's great research for my book.'

Dr Renata hesitated. 'But what about Ollie? This could be dangerous.'

'I'm coming too!' I said, before Aunt Caz could answer. 'So is Gasket. We have to beat Erebus Nyx!'

Dr Renata looked at me for a moment. Then she pulled a set of keys out of her pocket. 'OK. Let's go.'

Two minutes later, we were in her four-by-four, racing down the mountain.

## Chapter 28
## A Job for the Van

It was pitch-dark, and soon the four-by-four plunged into the smog. We couldn't see more than a few metres ahead.

Then we reached the mine – and suddenly we were in a pool of light. There were floodlights all round the car park and it was full of people. I recognized some of the miners – but they weren't going underground.

They were unloading turbine parts from the coal

hoist. And loading them on to big, flatbed lorries.

Everyone was working at top speed, and the first lorry was already full. I could hear it starting up, ready to drive away. Dr Renata gave everyone a wave and a thumbs up and then drove on towards the power station.

That car park was empty. The narrow, dirty streets around the power station were empty too – except for one old man, who turned to stare at the four-by-four.

Dr Renata braked and leaned out of the window, beckoning to him. As he came across, I saw the Leaf in his pocket, and he obviously recognized Dr Renata. I didn't understand what she said to him – but I knew what it meant. For a second, the man looked surprised. Then he nodded and hurried off.

Dr Renata sighed. 'He'll tell everyone round here,' she said. 'But that still leaves the rest of the city. I need to get the message to everyone else in the next half hour. That means driving to twenty different places.'

'We can do some of them!' Aunt Caz said excitedly.

'Can't we, Ollie? We'll take the van.'

'It hasn't got any fuel!' I said. 'Remember?'

'That's not a problem!' Dr Renata started driving again. 'I've got a can in the back. And a map of the city. If you could go to half the places –'

'Of *course* we will! Just tell us where.' Aunt Caz's eyes were gleaming. 'And tell us what to say when we get there.'

Dr Renata nodded. 'I'll write it down,' she said. 'Or – no, I've got a better idea!'

As we passed the power station, she stopped suddenly and jumped out. 'Back in a moment!' she called over her shoulder.

She knocked on the door of one of the little terraced houses. And then knocked again. Impatiently. After a moment, the door opened slowly and a head looked round it.

It was the girl I'd seen by the power station – the one who'd jumped out to distract me. Dr Renata spoke very fast, waving her hands around and pointing. It looked as though she was asking the girl to fetch her parents.

But that didn't happen. Instead, the girl grabbed an old coat from beside the door, and ran out, shutting the door behind her. She scrambled into the back of the four-by-four, and Dr Renata jumped in and drove off again.

'This is Ginny,' she said, as we zoomed towards the factory. 'She's going to come with you. OK?'

'Hi, Ginny,' I said.

Aunt Caz waved her hand and Ginny said something fast and fierce. The only words I understood were *Erebus Nyx*, but it was obvious what she meant. Dr Renata grinned and nodded.

'Ginny's parents work down the mine,' she said. 'They hate working for Erebus Nyx. But after tonight they'll be turbine engineers.'

I looked over my shoulder and saw Ginny grinning and nodding. 'Grio khazat!' she said, punching the air.

I grinned back. 'Grio khazat!' I said.

A couple of minutes later, we reached the turnip café, and the van was still there, where we'd left it. Dr Renata jumped out and handed me the fuel can. By the time I'd put the fuel in the tank, she'd marked up the map and handed it to Aunt Caz.

'This is what you have to do,' she said. 'Knock on the doors Ginny shows you, and let her explain.

Then the people in each house will pass the message around.' She reached out and tweaked the grio leaf in my pocket, pulling it up so the top was easy to spot. 'Come back to the factory when you've finished.'

'Is that where you'll be?' Aunt Caz said.

Dr Renata laughed. 'I'll be there all right. But you won't see me. I'll be right at the top of the tower, waiting to shout *GRIO FAROOZ*!'

I didn't know what the words meant – but I saw Ginny grin and punch the air. 'That's the signal to start the turbines?' I said.

'It is!' Dr Renata grinned. 'It starts the one on the factory – and that's the signal for all the others to turn on. Bringing new life to our city. Let's do it!' She jumped into the four-by-four and drove off to the other half of the town.

Aunt Caz's eyes were shining as she passed me the map. 'Come on!' she said. 'We've got work to do!'

She climbed into the van and started the engine. Ginny and I just had time to jump in before it pulled away from the kerb, setting out on its secret mission.

## Chapter 29
## Grio Khazat!

*Suppose they don't believe us?*

When Ginny and I went to the first house, I was expecting suspicious faces. Questions I couldn't understand. Even shouting.

But it wasn't like that at all. The man who opened the first door looked suspicious for a moment. Then he saw the grio leaf in my pocket and he smiled, as if we were already friends.

'Grio khazat!' I said.

The smile got bigger. He reached out and shook my hand. 'Renata?' he said.

I nodded, and Ginny started talking very fast, pointing round at all the other houses.

For a second the man looked surprised. Then he gave us a thumbs up and turned to tell the other people in his house. By the time we were back in the van, they were all out knocking on doors, passing the message on.

It took us almost an hour to visit the places Dr Renata had marked, but it was the same everywhere. Suspicious looks at first – and then huge, excited grins and people hurrying to tell their neighbours.

By the time we'd finished, we'd seen most of the city – and it was all the same. A network of narrow, twisting streets full of little houses. Every building we saw was run-down and dilapidated.

Except the towers.

We could only see the very bottom of each tower, but there was no mistaking them. They were all like the first one I'd seen, standing on their own in the middle of wide, empty squares. White marble walls going straight up into the smog, with no windows. Just two doors. One for the people and one for their cars.

I could see Aunt Caz getting angrier and angrier. 'It's not fair!' she kept saying. 'It's not *fair*!' And every time she said it, she banged her hand on the steering wheel and sent the van swerving from one side of the road to the other.

I was glad when we reached the last house. Ginny and I said our last 'grio khazat', saw the last surprised, excited smiles, and jumped back into the van.

'Let's get back to the factory,' I said. 'I want to see the turbines going up – and be there when they switch them on!'

'Me too!' said Aunt Caz.

She headed off, without even looking at the map. I grabbed it and called out directions, so we didn't get lost.

'. . . left . . . right . . . left . . . left – no, *LEFT!*'

Somehow we made it back through the city. We pulled into the factory car park just as the lorries from the mine were finishing unloading. The car park was eerily quiet. I could hear the machines running inside the factory, but the workers were all outside – unloading turbine parts.

Working in total silence.

Aunt Caz chuckled. 'The people in the towers can't have a clue what's happening down here. They'll have a shock when they wake up in the morning!'

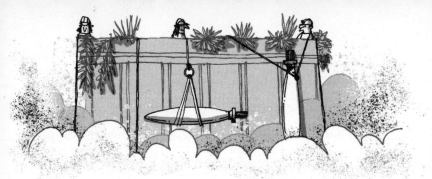

'If the turbines are finished,' I said.

Ginny and I climbed out of the van. Side by side, we stood and stared up at the factory tower. Ginny was so excited she was hopping from one foot to the other. But I was very still, watching the turbine parts being hoisted up the tower. The base and the generator. The gearbox. The brake and the shaft. The blades and the rotor and the hub . . . Piece by piece, they disappeared into the smog.

How many people were waiting to put them together? Would the turbine be ready to start by sunrise? Once all the parts had gone up, I closed my eyes, trying to imagine what was happening at the top of the tower.

That was a bad mistake.

I was so busy imagining that I didn't notice the noises behind me. Didn't turn round and see the vehicles creeping into the car park. Didn't take any notice when Gasket whined and tugged at my sleeve.

I was totally focused on what was happening up there in the smog. So was Ginny. And everyone else. We were all dreaming about the turbines starting. Until suddenly –

A blaze of light flooded the car park and a voice blared out from loudspeakers behind us. First something I couldn't understand – and then words in English.

'YOU'RE ALL UNDER ARREST!'

## Chapter 30
## The Standoff

Erebus Nyx had arrived.

He climbed out of a huge, gleaming car and stood staring at us all. Dozens of soldiers in helmets and body armour marched into place behind him, holding their shields together in a long, unbroken line. It wasn't hard to guess who they were.

The city guards.

Their faces were hidden by their helmet visors and they stood totally, scarily still. Like robots. Gasket growled, and bared his teeth, and I grabbed his tool-belt lead so he couldn't charge at them.

Mr Nyx walked forward, glaring at me. His face wasn't friendly now. It was pale with fury, and his eyes were hard and cold. 'I trusted you!' he said.

'No you didn't!' I shouted. 'You tricked me! You told lies about the People of the Leaf. And you put a secret mic on Gasket's collar.'

'You're a *bad man*!' Aunt Caz yelled through the van window.

Erebus Nyx ignored her. He kept staring at me, and his face twisted into a sneer. 'Stupid boy. You could have been on my side – helping to control the city. But you chose to join the losers and now you must pay the price. Guards – arrest him!'

Two of the guards took a step towards me. Ginny moved closer, so we were standing shoulder to shoulder – and then another voice rang out, from way above our heads. 'DON'T TOUCH THE BOY!'

Everyone turned round to look.

Dr Renata came abseiling down the factory

tower. The moment her feet touched the ground, she unclipped her harness and strode up to Erebus Nyx. Standing opposite him, she looked small and old – barely half his size – but her voice was strong and steady. It carried across the silent car park.

'Your time is over, Erebus Nyx! You've made a fortune by exploiting this city. You've grown rich by keeping your workers poor. You've poisoned the air and killed the plants. Feasted on hothouse fruit in your tower while the rest of us have had to live on turnips. The People of the Leaf say, "Enough!"

197

There's a better way to run our city. When we turn on our wind turbines, your day will be over!'

Erebus Nyx smiled. A smug, unpleasant smile. 'Think again!' he said. 'I and my family run this city. And that's how it's going to stay.'

He turned round and spoke to the city guards, pointing at Dr Renata. Then at the crowd. And then higher, up into the smog – not just pointing, but smashing his fist into the palm of his other hand, again and again and again.

I didn't understand the words he was saying. But I knew what they meant. He was telling the city guards to smash the turbines.

The captain of the guards saluted smartly, then turned round and shouted an order. Half a dozen guards marched forward, pushing people out of the way and forming a line in front of the tower. One of them reached up and slashed at the abseiling rope, cutting it off way above his head.

Now Dr Renata couldn't get back up the tower. How was she going to give the starting signal?

She tried. Throwing her head back, she shouted, at the top of her voice. 'GRIO FAROOZ!' But it was no use. We all knew the sound hadn't reached the top of the tower.

And without that signal, the turbines would never start.

It felt like the end of everything. Ginny looked as if she was going to burst into tears and Aunt Caz was hiding her face in her hands. Dr Renata's wonderful plan was ruined and the People of the Leaf had failed. I shut my eyes, to block it all out.

But Gasket kept nudging me.

I opened my eyes again and looked down. 'Stop it!' I hissed.

He didn't. He edged closer, as if he was trying to push his nose right into my pocket. What was he doing?

I took a step away from him. Without looking, because I was watching the guards surround Dr Renata. She couldn't possibly escape. It was the end of everything.

And then Gasket started nudging again – and I remembered what I'd got in my pocket.

We had one chance left!

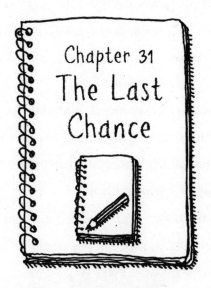

## Chapter 31
## The Last Chance

Everyone was watching Dr Renata now. Waiting to see what orders Erebus Nyx would give the guards. That gave me the chance I needed. But I couldn't do it all by myself.

I nudged Ginny, putting my finger to my lips so she didn't speak. Then I found the notebook and pen in my toolbelt. Very quietly, I tore a page out of the notebook. I mimed writing on the paper – to show Ginny what I wanted her to do – and then whispered what I wanted her to write.

She looked puzzled, but she started writing. I couldn't read the words – I couldn't even read the *letters* – but I knew what they said.

*Grio farooz!*

While she was writing, I glanced up quickly, to make sure no one was watching us, and then I took out what was in my pocket. Gasket licked my hand, staring at what I was holding.

The mini-drone.

I checked it quickly. Nothing was loose or bent. So my plan *might* work. If I had enough charge on my phone.

Ginny gave me the message and I folded it up and tucked it into the top of the drone, next to the tiny camera. Then I took out my phone, started the drone and held it flat on the palm of my hand.

For a couple of heart-stopping seconds, I was terrified someone would hear it. But the captain of the guards was shouting orders and the other guards were marching to surround the People of the Leaf, clattering their shields together threateningly. The noise camouflaged the sound as the drone warmed up, took off, and disappeared into the smog.

I watched the camera pictures on my phone. At first they were totally blank. Just the thick grey-white of smog. *Hurry! Hurry!* I thought. Soon the guards would march into the factory and up the tower, to start smashing the turbine.

Then, after almost half a minute – twenty-eight agonizing seconds – the drone came out of the smog. The pictures it sent back showed the turbine, gleaming in the faint light of dawn! Concentrating hard, I steered the drone towards it, aiming for the nearest person I could see. Willing her to notice it. Willing her to find the message.

For a second, she tried to brush the drone away, as if it was an insect. Then she realized what it was, and snatched it out of the air.

*Find the paper*, I thought. *Quickly!*

She did! Unfolding it, she read the message – and started calling to the others, straight away. A second later, I saw the turbine begin to turn. And that was the signal for all the others! They would all be starting up now, right across the city!

Ginny leaned over to look at the phone. We grinned at each other and watched the turbines. Just for a moment, I felt triumphant. We'd done it!

Then reality hit me. Yes, we'd got the turbines to start. But that wouldn't save them from the guards. As soon as Erebus Nyx had dealt with the people on the ground, he would send the guards up this tower and all the other towers in the city. The People of the Leaf wouldn't be able to stop them. By sunset, the turbines would all be smashed, before they'd had a chance to show what they could do.

Already, the guards had formed a circle round the people in the factory car park. Now they started herding them towards the centre, where Dr Renata stood facing Erebus Nyx. Everyone was shouting protests and some of the children were crying.

I watched for as long as I could bear to. Then I turned off my phone, in despair, and tilted my head back to glare at the thick, horrible smog. It was going to win after all. The turbines would be torn down and the smog would get thicker and thicker, and . . .

The smog . . .

The turbines . . .

**???**

**!!!**

Suddenly, I realized people had stopped shouting. I looked back at the car park and saw the crowd watching in horror as the captain of the guards walked slowly towards Dr Renata. His face was grim.

'No!' I yelled. 'Leave her alone! Look!' I pointed up the tower, shouting at the top of my voice. 'Look up there!'

Chapter 32
Turbine
Power!

What I could see was – the turbine!

It wasn't clear yet, just a vague shape, looming through the smog. But it was definitely *visible*. The night was over, the sun was rising – and *the smog was getting thinner*!

And that meant –

'The turbine is lifting the smog!' I shouted. 'And it's blowing away!'

Most people couldn't understand what I was

saying. But they didn't need to understand. When they saw me pointing, they looked up – and saw the turbine for themselves. For a second, there was a stunned, disbelieving silence. Then a huge cheer rang across the car park.

Dr Renata gave a small, satisfied nod. 'I wasn't sure,' she murmured. 'But I hoped that would happen.' She turned to the captain of the guards and stretched out her arms, waiting for him to handcuff her.

The handcuffs were hanging from the captain's belt. As he reached to unclip them, he glanced up, scornfully, to see why people were cheering.

When he saw the turbine, his hand stopped moving.

For a long moment, he stared up, watching it get clearer every second. When he looked back at Dr Renata, his face had changed. He unstrapped his helmet and threw it on the ground.

'Grio khazat!' he shouted. *I choose the Leaf!*

Suddenly, all the guards were doing the same

thing. Their helmets clattered to the ground and their voices echoed across the car park.

'Grio khazat!'

'Grio khazat!'

'Grio khazat!'

People started smiling and laughing and hugging each other, staring up at the turbines and then back at the guards.

The only person who wasn't smiling was Erebus Nyx. He stood in the middle of the car park, glowering at Dr Renata. He took a step towards her – and Gasket growled and bared his teeth.

And then something totally unexpected happened.

A huge, shiny black car sped into the car park and stopped, with a loud squeal of brakes. I just had time to notice the numberplate – EN 2 – before the doors flew open and children started tumbling out. First the little girl I'd seen on Erebus Nyx's balcony. Then one, two, three, four, *five* more!

Ginny laughed as they raced across the car park, screaming with delight. They flung themselves at

Erebus Nyx, hanging on his arms and hugging his legs. Shouting up at him as though something wonderful had happened.

'He's got *children*?' Aunt Caz sounded amazed.

Dr Renata nodded. 'And look how happy they are! They're excited because the smog's disappearing – so they can see the city from their bedroom windows.' She laughed. '*They* won't like it if he pulls the turbines down.'

## Chapter 33
## Tomatoes and Treadmills

Erebus Nyx's children weren't the only happy people. As the sun rose higher in the sky, the rest of the Nyx family came down from their towers. His mother and father and uncles and aunts. Sisters and brothers and cousins and nieces and nephews. There were dozens of them, all smiling and laughing. Pointing up at the turbines and the sun and the blue sky that kept getting clearer and clearer.

And they weren't empty-handed. They came

carrying baskets of the fruit and vegetables to share
with the people on the ground. Peaches and grapes
and melons, grown high up on the towers. Apricots
and strawberries and kiwi fruit. Tomatoes and let-
tuces and aubergines and bright-red peppers.

They spread them out on blankets in the car park,
beckoning to everyone to come and share their cele-
bration breakfast picnic.

I couldn't wait! I'd been up all night and done a lot of running, and I was super hungry. I picked up a peach and bit into it. *Soon, there'll be peach trees down here on the ground*, I thought.

I imagined them, lining the city streets. And grio trees spreading across the mountains again until the city was full of peach blossom – and the mountain slopes were bright with yellow grio flowers.

I closed my eyes, trying to picture it.

When I opened them again, I saw something unexpected. One man coming out of a tower dragging a heavy weight. It wasn't a basket of fruit and vegetables. It was a treadmill!

Aunt Caz stared. 'Why on earth has he brought that down?'

The man spun round – with a huge grin on his face. 'You can have it!' he said. 'From now on, I'll do my running down here.' He waved his arm and pointed. 'I'll run all the way to the mountains!'

'Good luck!' said Aunt Caz. 'That's much better than running on a treadmill – isn't it, Ollie?'

I certainly didn't want to *run* on one. But I hated seeing that treadmill tossed out as if it was rubbish. A machine like that must be useful for something. I went over to look at it.

And suddenly I had an idea. If I could just get it into the van . . .

I started dragging it over there. It was so heavy I could hardly shift it, but Ginny came running to help. We heaved it into the boot and I took out my notebook.

Maybe I'd just make a few drawings . . .

Aunt Caz came across and shook my shoulder. 'Ollie! Don't start doing something else. We have to go home! I've finished my book and I need to send it to the publisher!'

I blinked at her. 'But – isn't it on the cave wall? What about copying it out?'

'Don't be silly!' Aunt Caz shook her head at me. 'That would take *days*. Dr Renata's going to photograph it and email the pictures. Now hurry up. We need to find a petrol station.'

'But . . .' I tried to think clearly. 'What about the quad bike?'

'Dr Renata's gone to fetch it. Stop wasting time, Ollie. We have to get going!'

It was like being sucked into a tornado. When Aunt Caz decides on something, she doesn't hang around. We drove straight to the petrol station and filled up the fuel tank.

By the time we'd finished at the pump, Dr Renata was just driving up with Ginny sitting beside her – and the quad bike in the back of the four-by-four.

Ginny helped me haul it across to the van and watched while I took the wheels off, to fit it round the treadmill.

I shut the boot, and Aunt Caz put an arm round my shoulders. 'It's time to go, Ollie.'

'We'll miss you,' Dr Renata said. 'Thank you for all you've done.' She leaned forward and tucked a fresh grio leaf into my pocket. 'Come back soon, Ollie. So we can have a proper talk about machines.'

Aunt Caz climbed into the van. 'I'll send you a copy of my book,' she said, as she started the engine.

Ginny high-fived me, grinning all over her face. 'Grio khazat!' She patted Gasket and he wagged his tail at double speed.

'Grio khazat, Ginny!' I said. 'We did it!'

Aunt Caz leaned out of the driver's window. 'Come on, Ollie, or I'll start without you!'

Gasket and I scrambled in – and we were off, roaring away up the hill.

When we reached the top, I made Aunt Caz stop, just for a minute. We got out and looked down at

the city. Its tall white towers were just as beautiful as before – but this time we could see the factory and the houses too. And the mountains beyond.

The forest around us was still dead, but new plants would be springing up before too long. And the grio trees would start spreading.

Aunt Caz grinned. 'Well done, Ollie,' she said as we got back into the van. 'Now let's go home!'

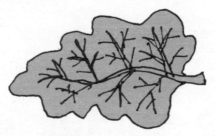

We did stop once more before we got on the ferry. At a petrol station. I wasn't going to risk running out of fuel again. I wanted to get home, so I could start converting the treadmill – into a wind turbine for the van!

I did try to draw some plans in my notebook, but I didn't get very far. Messages kept pinging in to my phone:

Still haven't fixed the boiler. You need to come home, Ollie! Dad xxx

Doing my sewing by hand – till you get back, Ollikins. Aunt Dionne x

Have to get up half an hour early, to WALK to school ☹

There was going to be a lot to do before I could start on that wind turbine . . .

Chapter 34

# Back Home

The van clattered up our road, swerved into the kerb
and screeched as Aunt Caz jammed on the brakes.
Everyone came rushing out of the house.

'Where have you been, Ollie?'

'We've *missed* you!'

'Have you been having adventures?'

'We had *three* jackdaws in the bedroom last night!'

'Did you meet any real spies?'

Mum didn't bother with questions at all. She just

jumped into the van and gave me a gigantic hug. 'Tell me everything you've been doing! Right now!'

'He's been *wonderful*!' Aunt Caz said. 'Faster than a rocket! Sharper than a needle!' She gave me the biggest smile I'd ever seen. 'You're a hero, Ollie!'

Dad put his head in through the window. 'Welcome back,' he said. Then he blinked. 'There's a *dog* sitting next to you.'

'He's my dog,' I said. 'His name's Gasket.'

'But –' Mum looked at Dad.

Dad looked at Mum.

'I don't think we've got *room* for another pet,' Mum said.

'We've already got Aunt Dionne's cat,' said Dad. 'And then there's Arabella's hamster and Zak's guinea pig and Lulu's ant farm . . .'

'Gasket's not a pet,' I said. 'He's a friend. Aren't you Gasket?'

He looked up at me for a second, with his big, dark eyes. Then he moved his head suddenly, as if he'd noticed something through the window.

'What is it?' I said.

Before I'd even finished speaking, Gasket scrambled over me, over Mum and out of the van. The cousins all squealed with delight and started patting him, but he didn't take any notice of them. He stood stiff-legged, staring up at the chimney.

I looked that way too – and my heart sank. There were *five* jackdaws up there. My jackdaw scarer wouldn't with cope as many as that. I'd have to redesign it . . .

Before I could work out how, Gasket started to bark.

He put his head back and barked and *barked* and BARKED! And the jackdaws took off in a terrified flurry, as if they thought he was coming to get them.

They flew right away, until they were just tiny black dots disappearing over the park. My uncles and aunts and cousins all started cheering.

I looked at Mum and Dad. They were both grinning.

'Oh well, there's always room for one more,' Mum said.

Dad nodded. 'Looks like he's already joined the family.'

Aunt Caz hooted triumphantly, and I jumped out to give Gasket a hug. I didn't need the jackdaw scarer now – but I couldn't wait to show him my other inventions!

# About the Author

GILLIAN CROSS was born in London. Writing stories for children is her main job, but she has done lots of other interesting jobs, including teaching, assisting a baker and advising the government about libraries and how important they are. Gillian has written many award-winning books, and her bestselling *Demon Headmaster* series has been dramatized for television. She has travelled round the world talking to readers about her books, and her adventures have taken her to exciting places like Belgium, Sweden, Brazil and Australia. In her spare time, Gillian likes to play the piano, swim, garden, orienteer (which involves finding your way round forests with a map) and, of course, read lots of books.

# About the Illustrator

ALAN SNOW was born in Kent. Before becoming an award-winning author and illustrator, he had many different jobs, including yogurt flavour mixer, tree surgeon (someone who looks after trees), and car/robot/wedding dress designer (but not all at the same time). He has written and illustrated lots of books for children, including a magical adventure called *Here Be Monsters!* This was made into a very successful cartoon film called *The Boxtrolls*, which was nominated for lots of awards, including an Oscar for Best Animated Feature film. Alan has recently spent time designing an ice-cream parlour, drawing inspiration from Willy Wonka's chocolate factory.

Ollie Spark, Gasket and Aunt Caz will return for more adventures!

Join Aunt Caz, Ollie and Gasket as they travel to a fancy food festival on a far-flung island! Extraordinary flavours and extravagant guests abound – and, of course, there are mysterious secrets that Ollie and Gasket must uncover . . .

More machines, mysteries and mayhem in *Ollie Spark and the Exploding Popcorn Mystery!*